OUR LADY
IN THE WOODS

By

M.G. MAGILL

ISBN-13: 978-1512262797

ISBN-10: 151226279X

DEDICATION

For John, my thanks for everything.

For my late mother, my thanks for passing into my DNA her own love of books and reading.

CONTENTS

ACKNOWLEDGMENTS

My thanks to Grainne Nelson, an excellent teacher of English in her own right, who did an initial edit of my manuscript and, similarly, to Barbara Waller, Margaret Magill, Joan Warwick, Marion Scott and Chris Philbin who did trial readings and gave me their opinions and suggestions.

Chapter 1

The whiteness of the foot stood out against the moist earthy soil and fallen leaves.

There was a pinkish, brownish umbra along the edge – a suggestion of something darker underneath.

It was perhaps the age of the foot, or its wear and tear over time.

It was almost posed.

The toes pointed downwards and curled together as in relaxed sleep.

It was a right foot but its partner must have been lying deeper in the undergrowth.

There was nothing to be seen of it.

The paper reported the gruesome find in the wood.

People who had enjoyed the quiet of the place though only a short distance from the nearby, busy road, thought twice about venturing there again; a walk they would have to do without.

What was the world coming to?

They'd always seemed all right together.

He was a bit older than her but not a huge gap.

You just never can tell what's going on in other people's lives.

Chapter 2

Philip left the main track. His eyes flicked right, left and ahead and, while trying to make things out in the greater gloom this far into the wood, he spotted the whiteness a few yards on. It seemed to come from under the tree that, towering as it did towards the crowded timber tops, was losing its grip with the ground. Its roots were standing quite clear of the earth that shelved into a lower track. It was too late for mushrooms.

There had been, though, an inordinate amount of rain that winter. As he approached, making more sense of what he saw shocked him to a standstill. He was aware of his heart pounding, his chest tight as he held his breath. He questioned what he had seen.

He picked up a stick to uncover the thing. He reached down and forward, aiming to keep a safe cordon between him and... he felt revolted as he nudged the stick against the foot. It was resistant to the gentle pressure of his stick's probing. He walked round the site to try and judge how a body might be hidden there, lying straight or curled foetally. He was excitedly curious and horrified at the same moment. From what he had seen of televised series, he knew not to disturb what might be a crime scene but he needed to be sure.

He advised himself to leave it to the police as he reached for his mobile phone. He patted pockets, irritated by not being able to lay his hand on it. Where was the damn thing? He thought he must have left it back in the car at the parking spaces for this track through the wood, criss-crossed as it was by woodland walks of different lengths. Consternation confused him. Which way had he come in? Which track had he been on? How was he going to be able to make his way back to this spot?

There was no other person he could call on.

He tried to calm down and reorient himself. "Breathe slowly," he encouraged himself. He let his breath out slowly and pieced together where he had been when he had stopped, leaving the track he had been following and coming down into this cabbage-green darkness. His mind was alert now to every minute sound but deafened at the same time by the pounding in his ears. Why didn't he just leave it for someone else to deal with?

He moved back to where he had first seen the foot, lying outside its duvet of brackish, crumbly soil and winter-wet leaves. He picked up the stick again and tried to lift some of the material covering what might be there beyond the foot. The stick wasn't strong enough and snapped as he applied pressure. He took in the ghastly wet whiteness of the foot and dared himself to uncover more.

In among the smells rising from the wood floor and the strong earthy sweetness given off by the wet undergrowth, he sensed something else, less of its place, odorous. His nose twitched resistance to the fetidness growing stronger from the pile. He darted short yards, here and there, looking for something to act as a lever. He was unwilling to stray too far, in case he lost sense of where he was and where the foot was located.

He tried breaking off a branch from a tree but the

wood was too sappy and strong.

Then, miraculously he thought, his foot kicked against something – a stone? A dense log? A metal bar. What on earth would that be doing here of all places? He grasped it with both hands and raised it from its trap of roots, soil and the suction of the earth made wet by the heavy rains. "This is more like it," he congratulated himself. He returned to the foot in its pile. He inserted the pointed end of the bar – an iron fence spike? He wondered where it had come from even as he used it to raise layers of earth, matted leaves and brambles from where the foot protruded. He dropped the mass almost immediately, sensing that what lay beyond the foot was intact and bare, denuded of any covering to clothe it against cold and wind and rain. He choked back a retch. It was evidently more than a foot.

He searched again for his mobile phone but he knew he had left it behind. A breeze was agitating the crowns of the surrounding trees. He was sheltered from the chill down at this level but was unnerved by the rustlings that focused on his aloneness and vulnerability. He tried once more to lift the carpet of interlaced vegetation, to work out whether the body, semi-revealed, was child or adult, male or female. Too much of it seemed pushed in among the raised roots of the tall fir he now rested against.

He took stock and planned how he would make his way out of the wood without losing the precise position of this grisly trove. There was too much to remember.

Which track had he left? Where? Why even – was it meant? Had he been singled out to retrieve this body for a more humane resting place? Had it been crying out to be found and its cries had caught the edge of his subconscious?

Philip determined then, with the light fading like a sigh, to make his way out.

He'd misjudged how late it had become and now the silent gloom made his attempts to leave the wood increasingly panic-stricken. He almost yelped with relief when the main track picked him up and bore him past a more recognisable set of markers: the picnic benches, the information boards for flora and fauna in this area, seasonal opening and closing times for the information centre. Then he made out the line of railings, black against the dark, grey light that edged the parking spaces. His was the only car there. He pressed the key fob and his spirits lightened as the rear lights welcomed him back.

Once inside he sat for a few moments, his head resting with his hands on the steering wheel. He sighed gently as if the responsibility he'd taken on was too great and he incapable. That reminded him about his mobile phone. He looked to see if it lay on the seat or had rolled off into the door well after turning some corner. None of the storage pockets revealed it.

Go home or straight to the police station? It would be too dark to take a team back to the place in the wood. Whoever it was, was dead already. Another few hours would not make any difference. It would be easier to direct the team back to the spot in the daylight. The shock of the find and its horror had made him more tired than he could have imagined, and a night's rest would restore him. But keeping the location in his mind plagued him, so he resolved to return home and ring the police from there. He felt for his biro and any scrap of paper, to jot down his key markers for returning to the spot. He found his appointment card for the next visit to the dentist but realised he couldn't see to write. He threw both card and pen on the passenger seat in exasperation and wrapped himself up in his seat belt, turned the ignition on and engaged reverse gear.

He arrived home and parked his car on the drive. Clunking the central locking with his key fob, he made his way to the front door. All was in darkness.

He felt for the keyhole, inserted his key, having turned it over in a second attempt to engage successfully. He reached for the light switch as he closed the door behind him. The light was harsh but the warmth from the central heating relaxed him. How late was it? Ten past seven.

The rush of sound brought him back to alertness. The click told him the kettle had boiled. He dropped a teabag and two sweeteners into the cup and watched the hot water colour from sherry into sepia.

Always dunk it twice, Margaret; it makes a stronger brew.

He smiled to himself at the memory. Philip brought what was left of the milk to add to the tea in his cup and relished the liquid in his dry mouth. It was hot but he kept on drinking until he felt the heat searing down to his stomach. He took his drink through to the lounge and dropped into his armchair, still wearing his outer jacket. He felt the awkward nudge into his thigh and supposed he had knocked the TV remote control into his chair. As he felt down the side of his chair, still holding his cup aloft to avoid spills, he made contact with the object and drew it out to rest it again on the well-padded arm. He saw the TV zapper resting on the arm of the sofa. He looked at what he was holding. It was a mobile phone. Not his, he noticed. Intrigued, he pressed the option key and the small screen lit dimly. The battery must need recharging. He spotted the 'missed message' box just as the power left the screen totally. He wondered what had happened to his own phone and where the charger was so that he could find out who owned the phone in his hand. He rested the unfinished tea on the small table and set off for the ground floor room they used for a study. Finding the charger in a desk drawer and plugging it into a socket, he felt for the connection hole at the base of the handset. Bingo! He pressed the switch to 'ON' and the charging icon blinked. He left it.

He shot awake. He was sweating. The sheets were clammy with sweat that had cooled. He tried to control his breathing which he was taking in as huge, noisy gulps like an asthmatic. His heart was beating in his throat. He'd been there, back in the wood, trying to pull the corpse out from its hole into which it seemed to have been cemented. Bits of the corpse tore off as he yanked and heaved.

Gently, gently. Take it gently, sighed the wind.

Piece after piece pulled off as his efforts became more frantic. There were bits of body littered behind him where he'd overbalanced with the frenzied force of each pull. He'd dug both hands into the ribcage to get more purchase and, with an almighty burst of effort, he'd pulled the rest of the body from its root catacomb. He'd looked at the scavenged face: Margaret.

He'd awoken shrieking and crying. It took time to calm himself and realise he'd been having a nightmare. He felt cold, got out of bed and went to the ensuite toilet and to put on his dressing gown. The light was on but he didn't remember pulling the cord. He left the bedroom to go downstairs and make himself a hot drink. The clock in the kitchen showed half past four. He didn't remember going to bed, undressing, any of it. What was happening to him? Why had the face in his dream been that of Margaret, his one-time secretary-cum-assistant and lover, briefly and mistakenly.

He shivered.

That had been over, as far as he was concerned at any rate, ages ago. He'd sensed Gayle was becoming suspicious and Margaret had become a bit clinging and then demanding. It had supposed to have been a bit of fun at first, for both of them…

Margaret had told him that her husband, Edward,

didn't show any interest in her physically any more. He'd developed some impotence problem and was shy of approaching anyone medical, let alone a psychiatrist.

When his lack of interest became fixed she'd started accepting offers to accompany Philip to far-flung meetings and conferences requiring at least one overnight stay. She would book rooms and make travel arrangements.

One of the other women she spoke to in the office had asked her how she got on with Philip. Had he tried anything with her? She had been surprised. There had been nothing other than business-like behaviour. Besides, they were both married people.

The other woman, Muriel, had looked at her overlong and smiled.

Chapter 3

At the bar one night after dinner Philip had asked her, "Fancy a double, Margaret?"

She'd looked at him, gauging a likely response when she replied jokingly, "What double do you mean, Philip, gin or bed?"

"Both, if you like, Margaret," he'd replied.

From such an inconsequential exchange grew Margaret's 'liaison dangéreuse'.

He'd suggested they take their drinks up to his room. She'd not known how to react despite the veiled suggestion coming from her in the first place. She hadn't wanted to make a fool of herself. She didn't have any idea about one-night stands and couldn't imagine the etiquette behind them. She went along with him to find out.

They chatted in the lift and, once inside the room, he put down his drink on the desk top and started to undress. He pulled back the covers of the bed and lay full length, resting his weight on one elbow so he could watch her. He made a gesture with his hand, inviting her to join him, chatting all the while.

His charming self-assurance eased her tentativeness and

she, too, removed her clothes, laying everything neatly over the chair at the desk. She saw he was mesmerised and evidently excited at the sight of her large and heavy breasts as she released their weight from the confines of her bra. She, who bore their weight every day, never knew what the fascination was, but Philip obviously felt it. He sucked in his breath as she joined him and immediately set to fondle and play with them, stroke them and tweak her nipples till she felt their increase. He held on to them and pressed them into her ribcage as he came into her from behind, doggy fashion.

He flipped her over and started hiding his face in their flesh, grunting his pleasure at them. She cupped their weight, first on one side and then the other, for him to suckle like a contented child.

That quickly changed to insistent adult when she arched her growing readiness against him. He entered her again and she clung to him as his rhythm quickened. She felt a great core of heat centred around the point of their physical connection and cried out as the cascade of long unvisited pleasure rolled out unreservedly. He relaxed while she enjoyed his efforts then concentrated on his own climax. With a satisfied exhalation of breath he rolled away from her, turned to switch off the light and was soon asleep.

She lay there in the dark, going over what they had just done and her own active part in it. She luxuriated for a while in her pleasurable betrayal of Edward but felt a pang of guilt that this reawakening for her was not with him.

All this time, she thought. Philip had loved her breasts. For Edward the sight of them, for some time, had only been greeted with disgust, as it seemed to her. If he loved her enough, he would go and see someone about his problem. She resolved to encourage him to do so once back home.

She came to early the next morning, feeling Philip's

hand exploring her breasts once more. She was still drowsily aroused from the previous night and turned over to face him, grasping his penis and encouraging his anticipation. He lifted himself on to her and she welcomed him into her. There was no languor about him this morning though. He was all mastery and precision and she feared he would be done before she was anywhere near ready herself. The tops of her legs were numbed by her straining against his weight in order to find the position that would recapture last night's pleasure – and there it came. She cried out as she gasped her thrill. He carried on to his own release.

They both laughed as he said into her ear, "Shush, Margaret, you'll wake the neighbours." As he rolled away from her, he slapped her thigh and said, "Right, Margaret, I thought you ought to have your money's worth. Make us both a cup of tea, then you'll want to be getting back to your own room. They'll be doing the newspaper round soon. Don't forget to dunk it twice, Margaret. It makes a stronger brew. You know how I like it." He winked at her.

She padded back to her room in a rough assembly of the clothes she'd been wearing the night before. She threw them on the bed as she went to shower. Under the heat of the water she felt the tingle of her last two encounters. She dressed for the day's conference sessions and went down to join the other delegates for breakfast. She didn't see Philip again until the end of the first session. He left a group of men among whom he had been chatting avidly and leaned over where she was sitting. "Why don't we give the coffee break a miss and meet in your room?" She nodded her assent.

He'd caught up with her in the corridor outside her room as she fumbled for the card in her bag. Once inside, he didn't wait for any ceremony before he was up against her at the door, easing her breasts out of her bra and pushing it up out of the way. He stopped to admire her anew as he undid his belt and dropped trousers and boxers to reveal his growing excitement under his shirt. He hastily pulled her skirt up around her waist and her knickers and tights down, to give him access to her. He lifted her bodily onto his hardness, using the door behind her to hold her weight as he started to thrust up into her. She wanted to laugh at how ridiculous they must both look and was breathless at the speed taken to be enjoying her, almost without involving her.

She wondered what the chambermaid, whose trolley she had seen at the end of the corridor, would be making of the rattle he was creating, banging against the door.

He pushed into her greedily and insistently. She had a pang of regret as he came quickly, before she had time to focus on any pleasure for herself.

He eased out of her and let her down. He pulled up his underwear and trousers and said, while redoing the notch on his belt, "Great tits, Margaret. Edward doesn't know what he's missing. I'll leave you to rearrange yourself while I have a quick word with Ashurst about the Fortiss business. I'll need to get my papers. See you at the reception desk after lunch. With any luck, we'll be back home in two to three hours."

With that he caressed her breasts once more and left. She rearranged her clothes, feeling tender around her breasts as she resumed their weight into the factory strength bra. She redid her hair and freshened her make-up. She looked at herself in the mirror and wondered whether she hadn't let herself be used and where this would all lead.

In the intervening weeks there was a lot of time assembling data and collation of figures from their survey trips around the country. There was a lot of pressure to have the report ready for senior staff in time, and all personnel were office-bound endlessly. She had hardly collided with Philip. She had wanted to meet more frequently outside of work. The absence of sex in her life for so long had given her an eager appetite now, but his move within the company had put a curb on the number of times they even saw each other across a conference table.

He never rang or e-mailed her.

Her life with Edward continued as before. She had tried various approaches in her decision to encourage him to get some treatment, but he had responded testily and had withdrawn into himself to a greater extent. Living life like brother and sister seemed to satisfy him but, for her, the gnawing lack of physical affection made her resentful.

Shopping one weekend, she drifted through the arcade and stepped into the lingerie shop she hadn't visited before. It was quite busy and she moved between the displays, searching for her own unique size in anything that looked feminine and frivolous. Her fantasy moments had given her a little, private core of enthralling memory and, as she moved towards the back of the shop, she was on the hunt for 'tawdry slut'; something to stand out against her white skin. And there it was… on a rail of obsolete bargains brought out for each sale season in the hope it would shift. There couldn't be many takers for it, being voluminous even in today's culture of enlargement. It was heavily boned and edged in frills of lace. The red satin, what there was of it, suited her present mood and she asked to try on the basque. The effect made her giggle to herself. This was perfect. If it never got a public outing again, it could be something she could try on in privacy. She wondered what Edward would make of her wearing it. She sighed her regret and frustration and took the basque to the till. The assistant smiled and asked her if she was planning anything naughty with it. She looked at the girl and said, "Yes, definitely!"

A fortnight later, Philip rang her at work and asked if she could be available to accompany him to Cumbria. The report was in the last stages prior to publication and her work on the background would be useful to him when the debrief to the compilers of the findings was given. She hesitated. His directness, so 'out of the blue', threw her momentarily. Wasn't there someone else who could accompany him? "No, Margaret. I want you to come with me. Will Edward be alright with that? Just the one night should do it. I'll get my secretary to make the bookings and go over them with you. Have you still got the files?" He didn't wait for her to say yea or nay and rang off. She controlled a spark of excited anticipation and left her current research to go and extract the files from the archive…

The meeting seemed interminable, with requests for this point to be emphasised and that paragraph to be given more prominence. Philip chaired the panel, referring to Margaret for clarification and chapter and verse to ease progress towards compromise.

Back at their hotel, set in the glorious Lakeland scenery, they ate a late dinner, going over the key points of the day's feedback. Philip would give humorous character assassinations against the people who had been most intransigent. They retired to the bar with piles of paper and folders. After what seemed like hours, Philip indicated he had had enough and asked if she'd take a sundowner with him in his room.

She agreed but wanted to offload all the paperwork in her room before joining him.

She drew the basque from its tissue and engineered herself into its tight corsetry. She could barely breathe both from the constraint of the metal bones against her ribs and her expectation of the effect on Philip. Even she admired the image of herself in the mirror. She locked the door, put the key in the pocket of her mac and picked her way, tottering on her high heels in the thick carpet.

She knocked on his door. It took a while for him to answer. He opened it and smiled an apology for keeping her waiting. "I was just ringing Gayle."

He reached to help her out of the mac and was spellbound by her appearance. He made her twirl, to take in the basque, the high heels and nothing else. She kicked off her shoes as he picked her up and threw her on to the bed. He followed after and buried his face in the great airbag of breast flesh plumped up and held firm by the corsetry. "My dear Margaret. You are asking for trouble going round dressed like this," he laughed when they were done. She lay cradled by his arm while he played with the lace and suspender satin ribbons.

"Do you love me a little, Philip?" she asked.

"Oh Margaret, don't be ridiculous. You know I don't. And you don't love me either. This is just great sex for the two of us. A perk of the job, a bit of fun to break up the crass boredom of life on the road. Besides which, I've got Gayle to consider and you have Edward. I wouldn't do anything to hurt Gayle." And with that, he turned his attention to the wonderful whiteness of her thighs against the redness of the satin basque. Two or three times more that night they tried to resolve their unsettled sleep. Margaret felt that this was perhaps a final flourish before the end. When she registered the rhythm of his sleep and gentle snoring, she slid on to all fours and felt around the room for her mac and shoes. She made her way back to her room and fell into a light sleep immediately.

She was roused, after what seemed like only minutes, by a muffled knocking on her door.

"Who is it?" she called out huskily.

"It's me. Who else are you tantalising with your affections here?"

She dragged herself to the door and opened it to see

him standing there, carrying two cups of tea and his room key, stark naked.

"You couldn't wait, I see. It's six fifteen," she said.

He sat them both down on her bed while they drank their tea. He reached to touch her glorious breasts, still framed in red and black. She drew away from him.

"Don't," she said. "They're very tender."

"You're an ungrateful tart, Margaret. I've been servicing you through the night and you slide off without a 'ta very much'. I'll show you tender."

He stood up from the edge of the bed and reached down for her ankles, pulling her bodily along the carpet till he could find room enough. He pushed her knees up to her diaphragm and pinned her with his weight. As he pushed against her, she screwed up her eyes in discomfort.

"Don't, don't. Easy, Philip, for god's sake!"

She tried to squirm out of her trapped position under him. He relaxed and looked into her face.

"Margaret. Let me, please let me."

He came closer into her face and, for the first and only time, closed his mouth over hers. She took it as a longed-for show of affection and welcomed his tongue, locking him there in suction. He had kissed her to cover her protests and moans but took the return of his kiss as permission to press on... and he did... and she let him. He wrenched away from her as his roar resounded in the silence of the room. He rested sweatily against the pillows of her breasts and sighed deeply, taking some minutes to breathe normally, laughing to himself now and again. He looked at her face, smudged with make-up and, ignoring two rivulets of tears that coursed to her ears, he said, "Margaret, you are a welcome companion on these trips up country and one great pussy in the bedroom department. I need to use your bathroom."

She lay there as he disappeared into the bathroom. She was shocked into a painful attempt to stand up by the shrill peal of the phone. She lifted the receiver. The night porter said there was a call for her from her husband. Would she take it? She heard Edward's irritated tone: "Margaret. Is that you? Where were you? I rang last night and you weren't in your room. I thought there was something wrong."

She explained that the previous day's session had run on well into the evening and that the meeting had reconvened after dinner and drinks. As she was talking she heard the flush of the toilet grow loud into the room as Philip came out of the bathroom. Edward heard it, too. "Is there somebody there, Margaret?"

She said it was Muriel Turnbill from Environmental Services. They'd booked a twin room to save money. She would see him later that day but couldn't say when. She was saying her goodbyes and trying to put the receiver down in haste as she felt Philip's skin against her back. He was breathing into her ear and licking her lobe noisily. "Ooops," was all he said and her shock of speaking to Edward was lost in the heat she felt under Philip's hands and fingers.

"There you are, Margaret, thoroughly debauched."

She swallowed uncomfortably. "I think he heard you."

He shrugged and smiled a lack of concern. "Will you lend me your mac so that I can get back to my room with both our reputations intact? I'll see you after breakfast. Will you drive us out to our meeting? I'm well and truly shagged."

The rest of the day spiralled downwards on the conveyor belt of their mutual exhaustion. Philip was not chairing this day's meeting and the slow progress of the early morning session prompted ever more crusty and acerbic interventions from him.

Margaret, who was known for her ability to retrieve from memory what had been compiled from previous meetings – the reason she had first been pointed out to Philip as a useful assistant in the current crisis – fluffed almost every request for clarification.

Her torso was sore and chafed from the damned basque and she saw her eventual return home stretching into the early hours of the morning. And thus it turned out.

Philip had given her a lift to the station in time to catch the last train south. She would be able to draft the panel's recommendations into a document which she could e-mail to him en route, and he would be able to put together the finished report ready for his meeting the next day in Sheffield. He hadn't referred once to their frenetic activities of the previous night. At the station car park, just as she was reaching for her bag, he stretched from the driver's side to caress her breasts, finishing, as he withdrew, by squeezing her nipple painfully.

"I don't expect we shall see each other anytime soon while this business is going on. Have a safe journey. Give my regards to Edward." With that, he accelerated away even as she was closing her passenger door.

His successful move to a new company had solved his growing dilemma of what Margaret expected from their infrequent couplings on these overnighters and put a curb on the number of times they would meet. She had, though, started ringing him and had written to him even, on one occasion.

He'd had to let her down gently but forcibly before the whole episode got out of hand.

She'd sulked for a while and made barbed comments when their paths had crossed but she seemed to have accepted that, whatever it had been, was over. He'd reminded himself to choose more carefully in future and had started paying more attention to Gayle. She'd made some probing remarks about his being let down by his latest lady friend but had welcomed his greater attention nevertheless.

Chapter 4

Philip tried without success to fall asleep again and lay still, feeling the surround of silence punctuated by his thoughts. He yawned, moved out of bed and felt his way downstairs to the kitchen again. He thought to ring Gayle and then remembered how early it was. What time would it be in Switzerland? An hour further into the day.

She had left for her three-month stint at the clinic in Basle. She had seemed a bit distant and standoffish in the days before he dropped her off at the airport. They lived in a perpetual turn round of requirements to be other than together – he for his environmental projects, she for her therapy clinics. When their free time coincided, it would, normally, be like a whirlwind romance cut short, inevitably, by the next case to be packed or the next list of what one had to do while the other was away.

This last time had been different though. He would look up to see her appraising him. When he smiled, she would look away and move out of the room.

She had shrugged off his tactile advances and turned her back against him in bed. He had put on hold any overture to see what might be wrong, thinking pressure of work or time of the month was the cause. He planned to fly over to see her in a fortnight when order would be restored.

He made a tea and took it with some paperwork back to bed. He drank the tea but couldn't make any progress with the files, finding himself at the end of a page of a report and unable to remember what he had read. His mind kept back-tracking through the woods to the spot he needed to pinpoint when he reported the body to the police later on. Interwoven with this piecing together and repetition were flashes from his dream, like something filmic coming out of his peripheral vision.

The radio alarm surprised him into the realisation that he had dropped off. He stretched and turned in bed, hearing the splatter and thump of papers sliding off the cover on to the bedroom carpet. The background discussion on the radio programme sounded like a muffled conversation heard through thin walls in the many hotel rooms he had stayed in across the country.

He showered and shaved. He dressed, choosing clothes that would suit today's trudge back through the woods. He'd looked through the curtains to see that it was dry; at least that would be helpful.

He ate some cereal and made more tea, thinking through his approach to any of the police officers who would take charge of this gruesome find. He collected his keys and laptop and remembered that he had left his mobile in the poacher's pocket of his waxed jacket, thrown in the back of his car when he had left work yesterday lunchtime.

He phoned work and told his secretary he would be delayed. There were no appointments to cancel today and she could get on with typing up the bits of the report he had left on his desk the previous day. He didn't say why he would be late. It frequently happened that he was diverted by some e-mail request and the secretary took it as a matter of course these days.

He drove into town and parked in a side street a short distance from the police station.

He presented himself at an empty reception counter and rang the bell. A man was sitting alongside, what Philip took to be, his teenage son. They both sat in silence.

The lad looked bored and resigned; the father tired and resentful.

Philip didn't say anything to them and rang the bell again. He could hear voices beyond the door leading off the space behind the reception counter. The door opened noisily and a woman officer came to the desk.

"Can I help you, sir?"

"Yes. Good morning. I need to speak to one of the detectives. I want to report something serious."

He gestured back towards the two sitting behind him to suggest they were not to be privy to what he had to say.

"Let me take down some details first, sir, if you don't mind."

She lifted on to the counter a pad of tear-off report sheets and proceeded to take down his name and contact details. She asked him for a brief statement about what he wanted to report. He replied that it wasn't something he wanted to discuss openly there in reception and asked again to meet one of the detectives. She seemed reluctant to take him at his word and pressed him again for some detail. He took the pad and pen and turned it towards him and wrote in the box: *I wish to report finding a body in Birkacre Woods*. He turned the pad back for her to read. She read the brief sentence, then looked at him for a moment.

"Just give me a minute, sir. I'll see if someone can speak to you."

There was a coincidental exhalation of breath from those in reception – each one loaded with its own meaning.

The lad spoke to his father in whiny complaint.

"Is that fella goin' ahead of us? We've bin 'angin' around in this place for ages."

His father told him to quit complaining, since it was his fault that they were both stuck there. Philip looked at him from his position, leaning against the counter. The man responded to his look by nodding his head in his boy's direction and shrugging his shoulders.

"Kids, eh? The tricks they get up to!"

Philip nodded his agreement, as if in sympathy with the man and, after what now seemed to him, several minutes, a door, built into the side wall of the reception area before the confined space of the counter, opened and a clean-shaven face leaned through the opening.

"Mr Innocent is it? Would you come this way?"

Philip ducked slightly as he followed the man through the door, down a corridor that smelt like a school he had been in and into an office, bare of any decoration, equipped with a table and some chairs.

"Take a seat, Mr Innocent."

The man closed the door and came round the table to sit opposite Philip.

"My name is Detective Inspector Morrison. I believe you have something serious to report."

He reached his hand across the table for Philip to shake and drew out a notepad from the drawer at his side of the table.

Philip cleared his throat and looked into the questioning face of Morrison.

"I was in Birkacre Woods yesterday afternoon after leaving work. My firm was involved in the development of the amenity and I led the project, so I take a personal interest in its use. It's handy for where I live and a good place to visit when I need to think through any new project I'm working on. I was following one of the lesser-used trails and saw something unusually white sticking out of the undergrowth. I took a closer look and saw that it was a human foot."

Morrison broke in.

"Did you disturb the site?"

"I had to lift some of the vegetation to find out that the foot was attached to a body. The light was fading quite quickly. It is a heavily-shaded spot. I thought it best to leave it to daylight and alert the police."

"Just this morning?"

"I couldn't see a few hours making a difference where someone is already dead and in an area that wouldn't have many people, or anybody for that matter, passing the site. It's quite a secluded spot. I'm only hoping I can remember my way back there."

Morrison raised an eyebrow quizzically.

"Well, Mr Innocent, perhaps you would show me. Did you walk here?"

"No, I'm parked just beyond the station in one of the side streets."

"I'll get a couple of men and alert SOCOs and we'll follow you… to where exactly?"

"There's a visitor car park at the north end of the woods along Birkacre Road. I can wait for you there."

"Give me half an hour to make some arrangements this end and we'll meet in the car park. You won't, I presume, Mr Innocent, have mentioned this to the press."

"Indeed not!"

Philip sat in the car, looking out towards the access gate to the trails. He rehearsed in his mind the route back to the spot where the body was and reassured himself that he hadn't dreamt the events of the previous day. As he was musing on all this, he heard the crunch of tyres on gravel and turned to see two cars pull in to the car park, one unmarked and the other a police car. They parked either side of his own car.

Philip got out and waited for the occupants of the two cars to reveal themselves.

Morrison had a female plain clothes officer in tow, and two uniformed officers emerged from the police vehicle.

"This is a colleague of mine, Mr Innocent. Detective Constable Gillibrand."

"Detective." Philip acknowledged her with a nod.

"Constables Winch and Thomas will help us, too."

Philip nodded at the other two men.

"Lead the way, Mr Innocent."

Philip set off with the others clustered in his wake. It was lighter today and he quickly ticked off mentally the markers to the lower trail access gate in the railings, Visitor Centre information board; flora and fauna board; the picnic benches beyond.

These were along the main track he had been following the previous day and he concentrated on locating the point at which he had decided to drop down to the less frequently visited lower trail. It was more overgrown than the more popular, open trails and he had made a mental note to contact the trustees and get them to organise some remedial work. Now, Philip was setting a brisk pace and he was aware of the lessening of communication behind him and more emphasis on hard breathing.

"Could you slow down a bit, Mr Innocent? We don't want to miss anything along the route."

"I just want to be sure and find the spot again,

Inspector."

He noticed, just then, the three tall pines among the more deciduous trees in this section that marked the divergence from the wider path to the narrower, root-strewn walkway.

"Mind you don't trip!"

He picked his way carefully himself, the slope of the ground dropping in stages and the light diminishing as the evergreen trees joined foliages to mask out the daylight.

"We're nearly there now, I think. There's a lake beyond if you keep on walking to the right and a trail that leads you up to the top of Birkacre Hill, but I'll be keeping to the left, so let's press on, shall we?"

He checked his watch. They had been walking for twenty minutes. Another five should bring them to the spot.

The vegetation grew more dense, and the light levels even lower. Philip was aware of the smack and crack of footfalls following his lead. He could feel the growing tingle at the back of his neck as he approached what he remembered as a steep drop in the walkway, followed almost immediately by a narrow rise hemmed in by trees and bushes on either side. He stood at the height of the rise and recognised the wide, sweeping bowl shape below him. He turned to the others and addressed them nervously.

"This is it. We're here."

Morrison moved ahead of the rest and came up close behind Philip to get a view but the space was too narrow for them both to stand alongside each other and Morrison had to raise himself on tiptoe to see over Philip's shoulder, to where he was indicating the lowest point of the bowl. Philip gestured to Morrison and the rest to follow him as he guided the group down through the clumps of brambles and fallen trunks to where a tree of huge girth was balanced precariously against the slope of the land, with its exposed roots holding up the height and spread of the tree into the canopy of growth covering the hillside. A dense mass of brambles formed a skirt around the thick, cable-like roots of the tree. Philip moved slowly along the edge of the skirt of brambles until he reached a small arch in the interlacing of vicious bramble shoots.

He pointed to show Morrison where something peculiarly white stuck out from what could have been an opening to a tent or a burrow for a hibernating animal.

Morrison and the others gathered round. Philip stood back to let them take in the detail of the spot. Even in the dim light, there was no doubting they were looking at something human and dead. Philip moved around the back of them to where he had let fall the iron railing the previous day. He brought it round in front of the group and showed them the beginnings of the rest of the body as he used the spike to lift up the mat of vegetation from on top of the foot and the leg it was attached to.

"Where did you get that?"

"It was underfoot yesterday when I was looking for something to act as a lever."

"It's strange that it should be here. We haven't seen any railings since we came in."

"Yes, Inspector. That's what I thought."

Morrison took out his mobile and swore to himself when he couldn't get a signal to make a call.

"Damn! Which is nearer, Mr Innocent, the lake or the car park?"

"You'll probably have to go back to the car park. I think it's too early in the season for the Visitor Centre to be open."

Morrison started to issue instructions to Gillibrand and

the two uniformed officers for securing the site and contacting forensic and scene of crime personnel.

"Beryl, get on to Dayton and find out if he can get down here ASAP! Get on to SOCOs again, as well, and, Mr Innocent, perhaps you will show us the route back. You stay here, Winch. Thomas, you'd better come back with us and get the tape to close off this bowl. It's going to be a long day."

Morrison left Winch to guard the site and followed the trio heading back to the car park. He caught up with them alongside the picnic tables.

"Mr Innocent, could I have a few words with you?"

"Of course, Inspector. I'll help in any way I can."

While the other two got on with the jobs assigned to them, Morrison invited Philip to sit in his car.

"I'm going to have to ask you to come into the police station to have your fingerprints taken, Mr Innocent. You've handled that railing and, so close to the body, suggests to me that it might be part of the crime scene."

"Of course. I can call on my way back to work. I told my secretary I would be out of the office this morning."

"Can I ask you what you were doing in that part of the woods, sir?"

"Well, I think I mentioned the fact that I led the development of the woods as an amenity and I drop in to see how it's being used and managed. It's some time since I'd visited that particular lower trail and, seeing how overgrown it had become, I thought I'd check it out. During the week it's quieter. You get the occasional mountain biker. I find it a good place to visit if I'm working on something new. My wife, Gayle, works away from home for extended periods, so I tend to come here more often then.

"What does she do, sir?"

"She's a therapist – sexual dysfunction. She does a three-month stint at a clinic in Switzerland alongside her referral work for the NHS in this country."

"Is she away at the moment?"

"She just left yesterday, the fourteenth. I dropped her off at the airport before checking over Birkacre Woods. I'm due to go out for a weekend in a few days' time."

"It can't be easy keeping relationships going like that, sir."

"It can be a bit like ships passing in the night, particularly if I'm working away, too. But we're alright. Time together is important and we make the most of it when our work schedules allow it."

"Who looks after the children, then?"

"We don't have any. I can't. I had mumps when I was a teenager and it left me sterile."

"I see. I'm sorry about that, sir."

Another car pulled into the car park. Morrison looked at it.

"Oh good! That'll be Dayton the pathologist. I'll just go and have a word. Well done Gillibrand. She must have caught him between jobs. Would you come, as well, sir? You can answer any of his questions before he gets stuck in."

Dayton opened the boot lid and took out wellingtons and got into a white overall before stepping into the boots. He then lifted out his heavy case.

"Well, Morrison. What have you got for me today?"

"It's looking like a body, hidden in dense undergrowth well into the woods on one of the lower trails. Mr Innocent here found it while he was out walking yesterday.

He'll show us back to the spot. Is that alright with you, Mr Innocent?"

Philip nodded as he checked his watch.

Dayton asked if the SOCOs had been called in.

"They're on their way, sir. I've asked them to organise lighting for the scene. It's quite dark even in daylight."

This came from Gillibrand who had wandered over to join them at Dayton's car.

"You'll be needing a hand with your case, sir. It's a twenty-minute trek to the spot."

"I see. Well, let's not waste this daylight."

A van drew into the car park. Four scene of crime officers kitted themselves out in white overalls and wellingtons. Thomas went over to them to brief them about the location. There was a disgruntled acceptance that they would need two or even three trips to take all their equipment down to the site.

"Dayton's already down there. I can help you with one of the spots to save time."

The SOCOs and Thomas set off with two spots and a trolley with cases and cameras. They would have to come back for the generator. Introductions were made once the bowl had been reached. They had to park the trolley and carry equipment up through the narrow rise and down again to where Dayton had earmarked an extra inner area to be taped off. Dayton was talking to Morrison, requisitioning a chainsaw to clear the space to access the body once photographs had been taken. They were standing in very limited daylight.

"Oh good! They've brought the spots."

He exhaled through his teeth when the senior SOCO said they would have to go back for the generator.

"You'd wonder how the body was concealed in such a

restricted space."

Morrison pointed to the railing spike close by where Philip was standing, taking in all this activity.

"Mr Innocent, here, found this when he came across the body yesterday."

Dayton asked him where he had found it. Philip looked around and tried to pinpoint the spot where he'd kicked against it. Dayton came across to examine the ground.

"I tried to break off a branch to use as a lever but it was too bendy. My foot kicked against it just here and I had to work it free from the undergrowth. The end was stuck in the earth but I eventually got it out and used it to lift the vegetation off the foot to see whatever else was there.

Philip showed Dayton how he had lifted the entangled blanket off the body. Morrison was looking underneath and shouted.

"What's that there, further up? It looks like it might be a piece of clothing."

Dayton saw it, too.

"It's something red. Upper body only, by the looks of it. The skin here looks to have been painted with something. I'll be able to say more when we've got the body to the lab, but it's looking female so far."

The SOCOs arrived back with the generator and set about connecting up spots to give more light. Photographs were taken and specimens collected and tagged, and the railing spike was wrapped, to be taken back to the lab.

A half an hour later a constable arrived with a chainsaw and handed it over to one of the scene of crime officers.

"Here, sign this, will you?"

The SOCO obliged and went over to Dayton to discuss what and where to cut in order to reveal the body.

"She's pushed hard back into the space here. If we can get round the back and start from there, we can peel back the vegetation and get a better look at her."

The combined, cacophonous noise of chainsaw and generator shattered the cloistered silence of the tree canopy and undergrowth. Officers stood away as chips of vegetation were thrown in all directions. They were finally able to cut a lid in the matted vegetation and start to peel back a section to reveal where the body was wedged and how it was positioned. The men cursed the sharp brambles that pierced clothing and flesh, as the team lifted off and removed to one side the cutaway section of undergrowth and bramble.

Dayton and Morrison looked at the wretched creature lying with the face turned away from them into the soft earth of the overhanging slope.

"She looks to be wearing some kind of corset. I wonder if we've got one of the local prostitutes here?"

Morrison looked at Philip who was standing transfixed at the image before him.

"Are you alright, Mr Innocent?"

Philip seemed to shake himself out of some reverie, swallowed and nodded blankly at Morrison.

"It's the shock of the find, sir. We're all affected the same way and not only with the first body we have to deal with. Come along. We'll leave Dayton and his team to conduct their searches while we go and organise a bag and a trolley for the body. You can go to the station and get your fingerprints taken, like I suggested earlier. Someone will take your statement, too."

Philip let himself be guided away from the base of the bowl. He was feeling shaken at the revealing of the body but even more horrified at the sight of the corset. It had instantly reminded him of Margaret and the horrors of his dream the previous night.

He shuddered and felt cold.

It was late afternoon by the time he finished at the station. He had left Morrison at the car park off Birkacre Road. The detective had reminded him about not saying anything to the press, as this was obviously going to be a case of suspicious death or murder. He had added that Philip would be contacted if any further questions needed to be asked.

Chapter 5

Philip dropped his keys and case in the hall and went to the kitchen to make a hot drink. The day had seemed endless. Looking through the window into the falling darkness outside, it was as if he had been shut out of the light all day. His mind went over the events. He felt weary. His heart went out to the person whose pathetic remains he had seen revealed in the dark confines of the base of the tree and he wondered what could have brought them to this unhappy death.

Turning on the radio to distract him from these gloomy thoughts, he set about preparing something quick to eat, feeling how hungry he was. He hadn't eaten anything since breakfast but, then again, neither had anybody else who'd been working in the woods.

He would ring Gayle after his snack. He checked the time and added an hour for European time, imagining where Gayle might be in her schedule. Recalling the way she had been before she left, he hoped whatever had been unsettling her was now resolved and they could look forward to the coming weekend. Giving her a mental hug, he set out his meal and ate it in the emptiness of the kitchen. He went back to the hall for his case and sifted among his papers for the notes on the next project claiming his attention.

Over an hour later he looked up towards the clock and imagined that Gayle would now be finished with any clients for the day. He fished for his mobile in his waxed jacket hanging over the back of the kitchen chair and sought out Gayle's number.

The interval between pressing the 'call' button and hearing the ringtone seemed endless. His breathing quickened as he waited to hear her voice. Then nothing. He let the mobile ring until he heard the voicemail take over. He left a brief "Hello, it's me. I'll try again later. Love you. Bye." An echo of his call resounded in the quiet of the moment. He was almost glad to be able to pace himself into hearing her later. Things wouldn't be so strained after his ice-breaker. He retrieved his laptop and gave his attention to that day's emails.

He worked on and, when he next looked up, he realised that over an hour had passed.

He re-called Gayle's number and waited. Once again, he thought he heard an echo of the ringtone. He pushed back the chair and, with the mobile still held to his ear, walked to the lounge passing the study they had on the ground floor. From inside the study he heard an echo of the ringtone he was listening to in his ear. It stopped in the study as the invitation for him to leave his message was given by the voicemail service recording. He saw the phone he had put on charge the previous evening. He spoke his message into his own phone and then ended his call. He went to lift the other phone out of the charger. He cancelled that call, too and studied the phone. He didn't recognise it as Gayle's but maybe she had changed it recently. She must have forgotten to take it. How odd! She was normally so careful with her last-minute checks. Then he remembered seeing her keying in a number on her mobile after he had dropped her off at the airport departures' layby. His shoulders and face gave expression to the strangeness of these last few moments. He flicked through the menus and contact numbers on this phone, looking for anything he recognised as associated with Gayle. Spotting the clinic's number, he held it onscreen while he lifted the receiver of the landline.

He punched in the number, waited for the international connection to be made and heard the first long introductory ring.

While they tended to work later over there, a check on the time showed that the clinic office would be closed for the day and, as he realised this, the German message followed by the English version invited him to leave his own message after the tone. He left something more formal this time, asking the staff to get Dr Innocent to contact him the next day. He was briefly annoyed not to get through to Gayle and almost immediately relented, thinking she might be out visiting a colleague or eating in any one of their favourite bistros when they met up there: Zum Wohl, maybe, or the little Bierstube in Hansgasse with its cobbled street and the alleyways running off it that opened up into flower-filled courtyards in the summer months.

He set the phone down on the desk and, taking his own into the lounge, sat in the chair and switched on the TV. It was late, and he looked for a news programme to catch up on whatever else had been happening in the world or his part of it. There was nothing about his find in Birkacre Woods. It was probably too early in the investigation for any local newshound to have picked up on the radar that there was a good story in the offing. Morrison would probably keep the media at bay for as long as he could. Philip decided to call it a day and went up to bed.

The alarm sounding found him tetchy from a disturbed night's sleep. He went to work and hoped by the end of the morning to have heard from Gayle.

The morning was spent contacting clients and reporting on progress with the start-up of their differing projects or receiving feedback and emendations to work at various stages of completion. Just before he broke for a lunch break, his mobile rang. He grasped it in excited anticipation of hearing Gayle at the other end. It was not Gayle.

An accented voice introduced herself as Frau Schied from the Staatsklinik, Basle, wanting to speak to Mr Innocent.

"Speaking," he replied.

"Herr Innocent, ach gut. We got your message on ze answering machine but we are a little confused. Doktor Innocent is not due to come for our patients till ze seventeenth."

Chapter 6

Gayle felt a heaviness descend on her chest as she waved tentatively to Philip, making his way from the drop-off bay, around the one-way system and the off to the main exit. She almost sobbed as the rear lights of his car disappeared into the twilight. She had felt locked in on herself for their last few days together. He'd tried to keep their talk light, skirting around her resentful unwillingness to engage in anything more than peremptory rebuffs.

She exhaled a long release of tension. He'd reached for her in bed the previous night and she had shrugged away from his touch. She had been torn, wanting to show her love for him but angry at his waywardness. She had wanted to accuse him there and then but thought it better to wait till she had spoken again to Rowan McCord.

She had met him only recently as a referral case to her clinic. In an introductory and follow-up session they had approached his presenting problem, through multiple layers of smoke and mirrors, to be erectile dysfunction and his abhorrence of sexual contact with his wife of twenty years. It was towards the end of their last session that Rowan McCord had explained his self-referral to her in particular. He had made an appointment with the clinic and insisted on meeting her because she had been recommended to him by someone whose opinion he held in high regard. He had appeared at her clinic, a tall, slim man, fair-haired and with a spectacular smile, showing slightly prominent but extraordinarily white teeth, all straight-edged and with hints of gold to his upper molars. Until she took down all his personal details, she had estimated him to be in his mid-fifties. His wife, he claimed, was a decade younger than him, Margaret by name. It came out without any preamble. Margaret had been having an affair with her husband, Philip.

She recalled the shock of the revelation, like immersing yourself in cold sea water at the beach; the drop in temperature between sand and sea suffocating your breath.

She had worked hard to keep the professional nature of their session ongoing, exploring the possibility of his imagining the affair as a justification for his own reluctance to engage sexually with his wife and transferring the responsibility for his negative feelings to Gayle as his medical counsellor. His blue eyes had fixed her firmly in a stare and his dazzling smile had seemed at odds with the slight self-deprecating shrug of his shoulders. He explained how he had found out that his wife had been with Mr Innocent in the Lake District on a series of fact-finding meetings with representatives of communities affected by the foot-and-mouth outbreak. Gayle felt her stomach contract into a painful knot but she tried to maintain her professional approach, particularly as their session was running over into the time of her next client. It was agreed that she would meet him before she left for her clinic in Switzerland. He would supply the evidence for his claim to include dates and places.

She had suggested the airport since she was due to leave for Switzerland but days ahead of her scheduled flight. This would give her time to absorb his information, check it, if possible, and face Philip, if necessary.

If Rowan McCord thought she would be leaving the country, she would be able to keep him at bay while she made her own checks on whatever he told her. That she was accepting of the possibility of its being true pained her but didn't surprise her.

Chapter 7

Philip was shaken by Frau Schied's message and asked her to double check that Gayle hadn't arrived unbeknownst to them.

"I can assure you, Mr Innocent, that we hev already done that."

"But I dropped her off at the airport only the other day."

"Perhaps Doktor Innocent was meeting wiz friends before starting her caseload for zis visit."

"Okay. Thank you for getting back to me. Will you ask her to contact me if she turns up, as she left her mobile phone behind here?"

"Of course, Mister Innocent. Goodbye."

Philip swallowed hard. His thoughts cast about for some kind of explanation. Had she mentioned meeting anybody before her stint at the clinic? He nipped back to their office to check any diary entries. There was nothing written but he spotted the flight reference set out in Gayle's handwriting. He decided to ring the airline and check when she might have flown.

He fidgeted while the assistant checked through screens of information for the reference number match.

"Here we are, Mr Innocent. You can catch her if you hurry down. She's due to take the 21.45 to Basle this evening. Do you live anywhere near the airport? She hasn't booked in yet."

"That's strange. I thought she left some days ago. Okay. Thanks. I'll come down. Could you have her paged for me? I should take about an hour to get there and parked. Ask her to meet me at your check-in desk. Can you arrange that for me, please? It's important."

"Yes, sir. I'll contact the desk with your message."

Philip checked his watch. He should be able to catch her if he left straight away.

He pulled into the short-stay parking area and collected his ticket. He almost ran to the airport main hall. Thank heavens this wasn't one of the bigger airports. He wouldn't have stood a chance. He made his way through the people queuing and milling, leave-taking and greeting. He saw the check-in desk but he couldn't see anything of Gayle. Where was she? She'd be cutting it fine if she wasn't here already.

He joined the queue that slow-motioned its way forwards. He craned his neck in each direction to see if she was waiting anywhere near. He couldn't see her and a mild panic took hold of him. His turn to approach the counter came and he asked the lady behind the counter if Mrs Innocent had checked in yet.

"We've got a note here to tell her to wait and speak with you before going to Departures but, I'm sorry Mr…?"

"Innocent, I'm her husband."

"Well, I'm sorry but she hasn't come through yet. Let me double check with my colleague… No, she's not booked in at either of our counters."

"When does she have to be checked in by?"

"She's got another half hour before we close check-in on this flight. Could I ask you to wait at the end of the queue and you'll be able to see her coming in."

"Yes, sure."

Philip waited and waited till the queue dribbled to nothing and he was left alone while the two assistants despatched the last suitcases to the conveyor belt.

"No luck yet? I hope she's not been held up in traffic or anything. She's going to miss her flight!"

Philip nodded at the woman and indicated he was moving to the main entrance. He stood there till the minutes ticked away her last chance to arrive in time. A tightness took hold of his chest as he tried to imagine where she might be. What was going on? *Gayle, where are you?* He almost shouted his inner appeal to the individuals and groups entering and leaving via the automatic doors. When it was obvious she wasn't going to come, he made his way back to the parking zone, paying his charge at a machine on the wall and getting his ticket stamped. He drove home in the late afternoon light and parked his car on the drive, unable to account for much of the journey he had just completed.

He moved quickly through the hall straight to where he had left Gayle's phone on the kitchen table. He scrolled through her contacts list and tried various numbers to find out if Gayle was with them or had contacted them over the last few days. Gayle's sister picked up on his growing panic, when trading possibilities for her whereabouts brought forward nothing useful.

"Have you rung the Cavendish clinic to see if she was working on extra appointments?"

"I told you already that I dropped her off myself at the airport."

"It's very strange and not like Gayle. Was she okay when you last saw her?"

"She was a bit standoffish but…"

"Well that doesn't sound like Gayle either. Had you had an argument or anything?"

"No, nothing like that. But she's left her mobile phone behind and I saw her using one when I dropped her off at the entrance. I didn't think she had more than one phone."

"What I suggest, then, is that you leave it for tonight to see if she comes back home. It will probably be something obvious that neither of us can account for, and, if she doesn't come back, contact the police tomorrow."

"The police?!"

"Yes."

"She might be in hospital somewhere if she's had an accident and if she's not contacted you she might be unconscious or being treated for something."

"Oh for God's sake, Laura. Don't make things worse!"

"See what happens tonight. Keep me posted, will you? Do you want me to come over? I could get a train tomorrow, maybe."

"I'll see if she turns up tonight. I hope to God she does."

"I hope so, too. Good luck, Philip. Get her to ring me when she comes in."

Chapter 8

Night passed into early morning. Philip tossed and turned relentlessly. Nothing reasonable answered his question about where Gayle might be. At 5 a.m. he got up to make some tea and toast to break the cycle of restlessness. He decided he would contact the Cavendish clinic again and press for possibilities that Gayle hadn't mentioned to him. He would reorganise his morning agenda and go to the clinic in person and speak to someone senior.

He approached the reception area and introduced himself, asking to speak to his wife. The assistant on the desk looked up some schedule and told him that Dr Innocent wasn't due in for another three months. The look she gave him spoke of her surprise that he didn't already know that.

He asked to speak to the departmental consultant.

"She'll be busy with a client. I'll just check for you."

The receptionist went off down a corridor past a series of doors. She returned with an invitation for him to speak to Mrs Cavendish, the senior consultant. Philip followed the woman back down the corridor and was shown into a consulting room.

"Pleased to meet you, Mr Innocent. What can I help you with?"

Philip gave the bare bones of his reason for coming to the clinic. Mrs Cavendish looked concerned.

"Gayle made all her normal arrangements to start her Swiss clinic on the seventeenth."

Philip asked when Gayle had last seen patients. Mrs Cavendish checked her computer roster and advised him that she'd seen a client on the morning of the fourteenth.

"That's what I thought. I gave her a lift to the airport that afternoon. I checked with the Swiss clinic who confirmed the seventeenth as the start of her appointments with them, but the airline only had her booking for a flight on the seventeenth that she didn't turn up for."

"That's certainly sounding strange. Have you checked with the police or local hospitals in case she's had an accident?"

"That'll be where I am going next. I was hoping you could fill in the time difference with some sort of explanation."

"I'm sorry I can't help you. Please let me know either way when you've found out what's happened. I hope, obviously, it's something and nothing."

Philip made his goodbyes and left the clinic with an unfathomable weight on his mind. He decided to contact the police station where he had first met Detective Inspector Morrison. He arrived at the desk and spoke to the woman who had been on duty when he had given details of his grisly find.

"You haven't found another one, Mr Innocent?"

Philip thought she spoke in too light-hearted a fashion.

"No, I need some help. Do you keep a check on

accident admissions? I need to know if my wife, Gayle, has been in an accident. She was meant to take a flight on the seventeenth and didn't turn up for it."

"Just give me a second, Mr Innocent. I'll go and check."

After about five minutes, the door in the wall behind the counter opened and Morrison's head appeared.

"Mr Innocent. I hear you are looking for some help finding your wife. Would you like to come through?"

He lifted the counter and invited Philip through to an interview room.

"Take a seat, sir. Now how can we help?"

Philip sketched out the details, of giving Gayle a lift to the airport, checking with the Swiss clinic when he hadn't heard from her, finding her phone even though he'd seen her with it as he was driving away from the drop-off zone and finding from the airline that she wasn't due to fly out until the seventeenth, and her not turning up for that date's flight.

"I can see why you would be worried. Give me some details. What's your wife's name?"

"Gayle Teresa Innocent."

"Date of birth?"

"She'll be forty this year, on the sixteenth of August."

"What does she look like? Do you have a photo?"

"She's about five foot five, blue eyes, brown hair. She was wearing a navy waxed jacket and dark blue trousers when I dropped her at the airport. She was carrying a black suitcase – one on wheels – when I left her off. I came here to see if she'd been in an accident."

"We are checking that now. Everything all right between you?"

"What do you mean?"

"Well, excuse me mentioning this, but one line of enquiry in cases of disappearance is to find out if there's a reason for one party running off. Sometimes they're running away from something and sometimes they're running to something… or just running. You know what I'm saying?"

Philip adjusted his position in the chair and hesitated with his answer.

"Do you mean was she seeing someone else?"

"Well, it happens, Mr Innocent."

Philip's retort came overloud and determined.

"No… nothing like that. I love my wife. We were supposed to meet up at the end of her first week at the Swiss clinic. I have a few days' leave owing."

"Do you have a photo on you?"

Philip reached into his jacket for his wallet and drew out a spare passport photo Gayle had given him. He handed it to Morrison.

Morrison looked carefully at the photo and then scraped his chair back as he stood up to leave the interview room.

"I'll just go and see if they've checked the admissions list. I won't keep you waiting long."

Philip looked round the bare walls as he waited for Morrison to return. His gaze lifted to the ceiling taking in the corners of the room and caught sight of the camera. He wondered if he was being watched. Morrison came back in, as he was wondering this.

"It's going to take longer than I'd hoped to check all the A and Es. We are stretched in the staffing while our other enquiry is going on. It's best if I give you a ring. I'll call you either way. Do we have your number?"

Philip gave his mobile number which Morrison noted down on a pad.

"Have you found out yet who the body is?"

"We are following a few lines of enquiry at the present. Apart from your wife, which you've just brought to our attention, there's no local person reported as missing. We might get some new lines of enquiry when Dayton has done his post-mortem and we get test reports. I'll get on with these A and E checks and get back to you as soon as possible. Is there anything else I can help you with?"

Philip stood up to leave, shaking his head.

"No thanks. You'll get back to me, won't you? I'll go to Basle for this coming weekend as planned and see if I can find anything there about Gayle. She can't just have disappeared."

"If you do find anything, you'll keep me informed?"

Morrison reached across a card with his number on it.

"Ring any time. I hope you find her soon. By the way, which airport did she… was she supposed to fly from? We could maybe have a look at their CCTV, in case our checks with hospitals come to nothing."

"Of course. Why didn't I think of that?"

"They wouldn't let you check the recordings yourself. It would need a police request, or a judge's authorisation in a civil matter."

"I see. Right. I'll just write some dates and times. I think I've still got a note of the actual flight reference. Though I can't think why that would be of any help, since she didn't turn up for it."

"Leave that with me anyway. Every little… and the rest. I wish you good luck with your search. We could do with some ourselves."

Philip and Morrison shook hands, as Morrison showed

him back to the reception counter.

He heaved his case out of the car and placed it at the front door while he searched for his house keys. Once inside he checked for post and went straight to the ground floor study to see if there were any messages. A red light winked and he pressed the button in a rush of anticipation of hearing Gayle's voice. It was her sister ringing to check on his trip to Basle. He'd let her know before he left of his enquiries with the Cavendish clinic staff and a check on hospital admissions with the police and of his intention to go ahead with the trip to Basle to make further enquiries there.

He rang Laura's number. She picked up almost immediately.

"Are you back? How did it go? Any further forward?"

Philip would have rather not had to explain his journey as a complete waste of time, but it had to be admitted. He blew out a long sigh of frustration before addressing Laura's queries.

"No is the short answer. I met staff at the Staatsklinik there; Frau Schied was helpful with a couple of Gayle's local Swiss contacts, but they led nowhere. No-one's seen her, nor heard from her, other than emails about clients' appointments for her first week of work, from days before she was to leave the UK. As far as Basle is concerned, she might as well not exist. I checked local restaurants and hotels, showed her picture to the local police to see if she'd been in an accident over there. Nothing, Laura. There's nothing to go on."

"What about the police over here? Anything from them?"

"I'm just through the door. I'm going to ring them to see if they've any clues at their end. In fact, I'll put the phone down and bring my case in. I've left the front door open… Ok, where were we?"

"Philip, you mentioned emails. Did she have her computer with her? You might be able to get some clues from the people she was sending messages to."

"I'd thought of that, but it's nowhere around the house."

"How about at her office?"

"It's unlikely that she would leave it there but I'll double check that."

"And have you looked through her phone calls?"

"I spent a couple of evenings doing just that. I've listed them all on my laptop – numbers, name, if any, date, time. That sort of thing, but I don't know for certain that it's her only phone because I found hers down the side of the chair in the lounge, and yet, I saw her using one at the airport."

"Anything for that date?"

"There was a call to a number I tried. Turned out to be an answering machine for a computer maintenance and repair business. So, maybe her computer's there with them."

"Did you contact them?"

"Yes, of course. I've left messages but nobody's got back to me."

"Do you want me to try?"

"You could have a go tomorrow, if you have a moment. I'll have to get back into the office and get some schedule organised to keep working projects on the go and try to free myself up a bit of time to pursue any leads, if there are going to be any.

Philip accessed his phone numbers file and read out the number for the computer firm to Laura.

"What will you say if you get through?"

"I'll pretend I need my files cleaned up, something like that and ask whether I can drop my computer in to their address. How does that sound? I'll get back to you tomorrow. When's a good time?"

"Just ring after six or leave a message, and I'll get back to you. Or text a message to Gayle's mobile. I keep it with me now, in case anyone makes contact."

"I'll give it my best shot. Try and keep your thoughts positive on this one, Philip. I'm sure we'll find her."

"I wish I had your confidence, Laura. Things are beginning to feel a bit grim after this weekend."

"You mustn't talk like that. One way or another, we're going to solve this mystery."

"It's 'or another' that's worrying me. Anyway, Laura. Thanks for your help. We'll talk soon, with some news hopefully. Bye then."

He put the phone back in its cradle and made for the kitchen to put the heating and hot water on at the boiler to get some warmth into the place and for a shower and shave. While he waited he sorted through the post that had arrived while he was away. He set his own mail to one side and concentrated on anything for Gayle. He opened three items – two brown envelopes relating to tax issues and clinic items and another inviting her to the local salon for a special rates fiesta for new customers. He made a meal for himself while waiting for the water to heat and sorted through his case for anything that needed washing. He checked in his wardrobe for a clean shirt for the next day. He looked for Morrison's number and decided to ring him. The phone must have been switched off, so he left a message saying he was back from his visit to Basle and was wondering if there was anything to report.

Chapter 9

Gayle phoned the number to say she was ready to meet. She emphasised she had two hours before she had to present herself for departures. He suggested collecting her from the drop-off bay and heading to some local park where they could talk and still be handy for the air terminal.

The silver BMW eased to a stop by where she was waiting with her case. He got out of the car and came to lift her case to put it into the boot. She hesitated but nodded at him to take it. They drove in silence. He was heading into the countryside surrounding the small airport. He pulled into a small car park beside a picnic area. He switched the motor off and turned to look at her.

"Will this do?"

"Yes, Mr McCord. We're only ten minutes away from where I need to be."

"Where are you off to?"

"I think I told you, Mr McCord, I have a number of clients to meet over at the Swiss clinic."

"Are there a lot of us with my problem?"

"Could we get down to why we are meeting like this? You said my husband was having an affair with your wife… Margaret, I think you said."

"I did indeed."

"Does she know you are meeting me?"

"I think not. She left some time ago on an ultimatum that either I would seek some treatment or she would go."

"And you didn't prevent her; offer to undergo some therapy and tests?"

"I felt so betrayed by her behaviour that I let her go, and then, later on, thought to seek out some treatment. Her insistent pressure to do something being removed, I felt more at ease with the decision to fend for myself. I made some discreet enquiries and your clinic was recommended to me, and you, in particular."

"Are you still in touch? Does she know you have taken this step?"

"No, she does not."

"That's a shame. Both parties being available for therapy helps consolidate a more positive outcome. The partner being aware and involved helps to revitalise what may have become staid and, in Margaret's case for example, unbearable."

"Spare your sympathies, please. The woman's a whore!"

Gayle felt an angry determination behind his remark, and his smile masked a cold, steely speculation behind his eyes.

"That may, of course, not be the way your wife would describe her circumstances. How are you able to say my husband was involved?"

"I became aware that her behaviour towards me changed. She started being away more often during the foot-and-mouth crisis, which was to be expected, but she became almost hysterical, at times, on her return from these trips with her demands that I do something, so that our lives could be more normal. I was under quite a bit of pressure myself at work then and I couldn't cope with her as well, being like she was; flaunting herself at me and taunting me with being less than a man should be."

"I can feel how Margaret's behaviour wouldn't be helpful in those circumstances but how does that involve my husband?"

"I phoned her at her hotel one evening. She wasn't available to answer. I rang again the next morning and she answered my call, but I felt there was someone in the room with her. She concocted a story about sharing with another woman from her department whom I'd happened to run into myself the previous evening while shopping for groceries at the local supermarket."

"And you said this at the time?"

"No, I raised it with her in the next argument that arose about my uselessness as a husband, even though she said she loved me and wanted to live a more normal relationship. She was shocked when I put my suspicions to her and the reason that I held them. It all unravelled before my ears. She wouldn't tell me the bloke's name, but I did some investigations of my own and put the name to her at a later date. She admitted that your husband was the man she had been spending time with on their overnighters over the past half-year and boasted about what a wonderful lover he had been. She meant to wound me."

Gayle winced inwardly but didn't interrupt his flow.

"We had a huge argument and she voiced her ultimatum. She left a fortnight later."

"I'm sorry things have turned out for you like this but I am still not sure how you come to be certain that my husband was her lover on each of these occasions. Margaret could have used his name to cover her activity with someone else, or from some professional jealousy or slight, or to create ripples in someone else's marriage. There are any number of reasons. He could act as a useful cover, if he was always part of the team touring the North on those fact-finding visits."

"As you say Dr Innocent… but…"

The word came from his mouth like a gentle puff of air with a tornado behind it…

"I wrote to him as if I were Margaret asking to meet up. The time together had been so enjoyable that she didn't want it to end."

"Did he answer?"

"He did. I have his reply still. Would you like to see it?"

With all her being she did not but nodded and held out her hand. He handed her a sheet torn off a notepad. She recognised Philip's department logo at the top of the sheet of paper and read the typewritten note:

Margaret, scrumptious Margaret.

We had great fun, but that is all it was from the beginning.

Fun for you. Fun for me, too. Now we are moving along different paths and all that is over and behind us. I have Gayle to consider.

Good luck. Over and out.

Philip

There was little comfort in his reference to her.

"Is that proof enough for you, Dr Innocent?"

She lifted her head towards him to see that same blank smile.

"Might I keep this?"

"Of course, Dr Innocent."

"What do you want from me with this, Mr McCord?"

"With so much interlinking our lives I would prefer you called me Rowan."

"That's as maybe, Mr McCord, but I have a professional relationship with you. I would want you to continue your therapy so that you could start again with Margaret, or somebody else, if the other has no life left in it."

He laughed out loud.

"Come and get your case. I'll drop you back at the airport."

As she reached into the now open boot for her case, he came at her from behind, where he had stood back to allow her to reach in.

He held something over her face. She struggled to breathe and squirmed to escape his strong hold. The more she struggled, the more she fought for breath until she'd absorbed so much of what was on the cloth over her face that she lost consciousness.

He lifted her now dead weight and dumped her carelessly into the boot, dropping the case back from where she'd reached to retrieve it. He threw her handbag on top of her. He breathed hard and closed the boot lid solidly.

"Now, Mr Philip Innocent. You are going to feel what it's like to have your world turned upside down."

He got into the driving seat, closed the door and felt its solid clunk, pressed the start button, heard the engine turn over, engaged 'drive', lifted his foot off the brake and pressed gently with his right foot on the accelerator. He allowed himself to smile again.

Chapter 10

He reversed the car into his garage, leaving enough space behind to open the boot. He aimed his zapper at the box on the wall, and the garage door rolled itself to the ground. He took the cushion from the back seat and moved round to the back of the car, pressing the button to release the boot lid. He lifted it cautiously, trying to sense any reaction from the woman within. Nothing to indicate she was conscious. He lifted out her case to give him space. Pulling her upper body back towards him and covering her face with the cushion, he pressed down hard and held the position until he judged her to have stopped breathing. His shoulders, legs and back ached with exerting the pressure from a standing position bent over into the confines of the boot space. He breathed in and out quickly until he could achieve an easier rhythm.

"What a shame, Doctor Innocent. I quite liked you. Your husband will have a lot to answer for."

Having regained some composure, he reached under her armpits and, with his hands joined across her chest, he hauled her out of the boot space. A heel caught against the lower rim of the boot space and, as he tugged and pulled, a shoe flipped off and balanced comically at an angle against her foot before dropping to the garage floor.

Breathing heavily again, he dragged her into a dark corner of the garage where there was an untidy pile of dustcovers and a tarpaulin. While she was still limp, he started to remove her clothing, jewellery and underwear. He bent her body into a curl among the sheets and covered it with the tarpaulin.

His heart was beating at a rapid rate against his chest and, as he stood up, he felt a slight dizziness. He stood still, resting against the side of the car until it passed. He reached down and grasped the clothes and underwear and stuffed them in the brazier just inside the door of the garage. He returned for the shoes and cursed when he saw that one had rolled under the back of the car. He got down on his hands and knees and, as he flattened himself against the floor to reach underneath for the shoe, his eyes looked beyond to where Gayle's foot protruded from below the tarpaulin. He tutted as he gathered the shoe to him and raised himself from the floor. He was breathless.

"There's no escape, I'm afraid, my dear."

He walked round the car and kicked her foot back under the cover. He felt in his pocket to check he had her rings and watch. He dropped the two shoes in among the rest of the clothing and went back to the boot to retrieve her bag. With this and her case he walked to the connecting door into the house. He felt for his keys and selected the garage door key, unlocked, pressed down the handle and pushed the door away from him into the quiet cool of his utility room. He manoeuvred the case and bag through the kitchen and ground floor to his study. The radiator rattled as the central heating came on. He started as the door bell rang. He took his time getting to the door, opened it and scrutinised the photo ID pushed towards him.

"Check your meter, mate? Mr Culpebble is it?"

Edward nodded. The man followed him through to the

garage. Edward pointed to where the electricity meter sat on the wall near the central heating boiler which was blowing noisily.

"Ok mate. Thank you."

The meter reader followed Edward back through to the front hall.

"Did you see you'd left your boot open?"

"Yes, I was emptying it when you rang the bell."

"Ok. Bye then."

And a goodbye to you, too, thought Edward as he retraced his steps back to the garage. He plugged the vacuum cleaner in at the wall, switched on the light and started to hoover the boot. When he was satisfied that anything relating to Gayle had been sucked up, he pulled out the plug from the socket, re-coiled the flex round the top of the Aquavac and trundled it back to its spot in the garage. He closed the boot, locked the car and made his way back to the study. He emptied the contents of Gayle's bag on to the carpet and selected out her mobile phone. He accessed her call history screen and deleted her last call to him arranging the rendezvous at the airport. He pocketed the mobile and searched out Gayle's keys. These he put into his jacket, checking once more for his car keys.

He parked the car on the main road and walked into the small estate where Philip and Gayle had their detached house. He turned into the narrow ginnel that followed the side fence of the property, turning at a right angle to follow their rear fence and those of the other properties backing on to a sports field. This dropped down behind the boundary of chestnut trees into a woodland walk through past a church car park and the entrance to a village primary school and up to a junction with the main road.

He'd walked it on his first of many recces and been spooked by a Doberman running loose off the lead among the trees and coming up behind him to seize him by the heel.

The dog's owners were making their way up to meet him, saw the dog holding on to the back of his shoe and called the dog's name. As it held on, they tried to reassure Edward that the dog was only playing. He was seething but didn't want to make too much of a fuss in case he became registered in their memory. He waited calmly while the couple took the dog's collar, attached the lead and yanked the dog away from him.

This time, in the mid-afternoon, there was no-one about as he went through the rear gate at Gayle's fence and approached the back door. He found the right key at his third selection among the Yale keys on the bunch. He walked through the ground floor, found the lounge, looked around it and selected the armchair nearest to the TV.

He put his gloves on and took Gayle's mobile from his jacket and pushed it down the side of the armrest and the cushion.

He laughed to himself and made his way out through the back door, locking it behind him. Still no-one about. He closed the latch of the rear gate and walked across the edge of the sports field to where it adjoined a path cutting through the line of houses that sat along the main road where he had left his car.

With the car once more parked in his garage, he returned to the study. He sorted through the contents of Gayle's bag scattered on the carpet where he had left them when the meter reader had called: purse, wallet with credit, debit cards, make up and sundry items he dismissed as useless to him. He took the cards and put them in his own wallet and took the rest of Gayle's paraphernalia to tip into the bin. The bag he squeezed into the brazier in the garage. He returned to the study and started to work through her suitcase. Finding nothing of any use to his current purposes, he zipped the case closed and hauled it up to his first floor landing. He dropped the ladder down from the attic cover and manoeuvred the case against his upper body, so that he could climb and push the case upwards at the same time. The weight of the case tipped over the edge of the opening on to the boarded floor of the attic space. He pulled the light switch cord and, having hauled himself upright using the roof trusses as a steadying support, he lifted the case to the darkest corner of the attic and then reversed his route back down to the landing. He looked at his watch – 7.30 p.m. Time to make something to eat. He felt suitably peckish after his afternoon's exertions.

Chapter 11

As Morrison entered the office he checked how many of his team had already arrived. Beryl was there, working at her computer screen. She raised her head and acknowledged his arrival with a mouthed 'Hi'. He nodded at her and went to the display board they'd started on the body-find in Birkacre Woods. Some of the photographs taken at the scene were affixed, showing the body that had been forced into the hollow in among the tree roots, now exposed after the men had lifted and removed the vegetation. The corset was shown flattened out and an additional, close-up shot showed the label – Beaulieu:Firebrand.

Geoff Waller ambled in from the kitchen area clutching a cup of something warm.

"Is Andy Raby in today?"

"Yes, sir. He's just at the filing cabinets."

"Ok, well when he gets back, let me know, and we'll review where we're at with this one."

He moved around the board and unlocked his office door, leaving it open as he laid his case on the desk, wrestled himself out of his outer jacket and hung it up behind the door which he was closing to when Detective Sergeant Raby appeared round the narrowed opening.

"Did you want to see me, sir?"

"Yes, Andy. Get the others together and we'll see what everyone's been working on."

"Righto, sir."

The small team gathered round the display board which looked under-filled. Dermond Morrison told his colleagues that they were expecting more photos and info from Dayton and Forensics. He went round each one of his team who reported on their activity and progress, or lack of it.

Beryl had been following up on the corset which had been removed from the corpse. Despite the time the corset had been hidden with the body, the item looked little worn.

She reported on her contact with the company who had informed her that the 'Firebrand' model was no longer made but were sending a list of previous stockists. Beryl had already made a start, ringing around women's underwear retail outlets and had made some internet searches on the 'burlesque', 'vicars and tarts' and fancy dress sites.

"The world's your whalebone then, Beryl."

"It's like looking for a hook and eye in a haystack, Sir. The trouble is, because it's not currently made, there's no knowing how long it's been hidden in somebody's drawer or sitting in the back stock of all these retail outlets. The only clue that we've got is the size. She must have been large-breasted – unusually so – 40G."

The three men looked at each other.

"Ok, Beryl. You'll carry on running the seller to ground."

"Right, Sir. I hope to make faster progress when I get the definitive list from Beaulieu."

Geoff Waller had been checking through 'missing persons' lists. Nobody was listed locally and, spreading the net within the immediate county hadn't matched with any white female in the 35-40 age bracket.

"Sir, who was the woman that you were contacted about? It couldn't be her by any chance?"

"Gayle Teresa Innocent, Geoff, is within the age range but she was last seen on the fourteenth of March; the same date that her husband, having given her a lift to the airport at Whitelake, then went on to find the body – or the foot of it, at any rate – in Birkacre Woods. He reported his find to us on the fifteenth, as you will know."

"What are the chances of that being a coincidence, Sir?" asked Andrew Raby.

"That remains to be seen when we get more details from Dayton. Once we have a photo of our lady in the woods, we can check it against the passport one that Philip Innocent gave me when he reported his wife's non-arrival in Basle where she was expected. How far did you get, Andy, with our friendly local sex workers?"

"Uniform have been asking around the local girls out on the streets, and I've requested checks by forces in Stoccelten, Landley, Buxby Bridge, Potswortham and Dubury Mill. That's just scratching the surface for now, until we have photo ID and more from Forensics. We'll need that before we go national."

"As soon as I get anything, you'll get it, too. Right, everybody, good hunting! Our lady in the woods needs your best efforts, as usual."

Morrison went into his office and closed the door. He checked his mobile and saw the text message listing. He'd been at a meeting with Chief Inspector Sandford at

Stenford HQ the previous evening and had switched his phone off. He pressed the option to call the number. Philip Innocent answered.

"Philip Innocent speaking. I tried ringing you when I got in last night to see if you'd had any information about Gayle."

"How did you get on in Basle?"

"No luck, I'm afraid. I spent the weekend checking with the clinic, contacts they supplied, local restaurants, police. Nothing. It's as if she never existed."

"Keep the faith, Mr Innocent. It's early days. Does she have any family locally?"

"Not locally, no. There's just her sister, Laura. She's a couple of years older than Gayle. I thought your call was her ringing. She was trying to find the name of a local computer maintenance and repair shop that there was a number for on Gayle's phone."

"You have her phone?"

"Yes. I have a phone. I found it down the side of an easy chair in our lounge the night I got back from Birkacre Woods. I'd seen her making a call when I left her off at Whitelake Airport that afternoon and I presumed she had another one – just for professional clients, maybe."

"I see."

"I talked with Laura last night before I rang you, and she was going to try and get through to the computer shop, get an address, then I could go and see if Gayle's computer is with them. It isn't here in the house. I haven't checked with Mrs Cavendish, the Senior Consultant at the Cavendish clinic. I don't imagine Gayle would have left it there, but just to make absolutely certain. She most definitely didn't have it with her as hand luggage which would be the case normally."

"Well you've been busy, that's for sure. Have you the number of the computer shop and, while we're at it, the clinic? Mrs Cavendish, did you say?"

Morrison noted down the two numbers and the address for the clinic. He'd get Geoff Waller to check for the shop address and he himself would pay Mrs Cavendish an initial visit while they were waiting for Dayton's reports to come in.

"Leave those with me, Mr Innocent. I'll get some checks organised from this end. Are you still on leave…? Oh, I see. Back to the grindstone. I'll be in touch if I find anything useful… Well, yes. If she rings with an address, let me know. It will save us doubling up the legwork. I'll be in touch. Goodbye, Mr Innocent."

Morrison went into the open office area and indicated to Geoff Waller, hunched over his screen, to come and speak to him.

"Anything for me, Sir?"

"I want you to find me an address for this phone number. It's a computer shop. If you get any result, ask for the manager and arrange to go and see him this afternoon, if it's not too far away. You're looking for something left in by a Mrs Gayle Innocent, before the fourteenth of March. You'll have to sign for it and then drop it over to ITDU in Stenport. We want access to view files. Say it's to do with a potential kidnapping. We don't want it sitting in their workshop for weeks. And don't forget to get a receipt."

Morrison turned to the clinic's number and arranged an appointment with Mrs Cavendish for 4 p.m. that same day. She would have finished with her client list for the day then…

"Good afternoon. Have you an appointment?"

"My name is Morrison and I'd arranged an appointment to talk to your Senior Consultant at 4 p.m."

"Just take a seat. I'll go and see if she's finished with her last appointment."

Morrison was led into Mrs Cavendish's consulting room. She came around her desk to shake hands.

"Would you like some tea or coffee, Mr Morrison?"

She indicated to the receptionist to bring coffee for him and pointed Morrison to a seating area away from her desk.

"How can I help you, Mr Morrison?"

Morrison showed his warrant card and was about to start speaking when a knock at the door heralded the arrival of refreshments. He waited while the receptionist unloaded her tray and then waited while Mrs Cavendish handed her some paperwork on the way out.

"I've come to ask you some questions about one of your team – Mrs Gayle Innocent."

"Yes, of course. Mr Innocent, her husband, was here last week. It seems very strange. What do you wish to know?"

"Just generally, how long you've known her; how she seemed to you before she left for Switzerland. Anything you might know of that would explain her absence. That kind of thing."

Morrison sampled the coffee while listening to Mrs Cavendish.

"Gayle, Dr. Innocent, has been working with us for about five years now. She's self-employed and does two contracts per year, in addition to her work with us, with the Staatsklinik in Basle, up by the Rhine, I believe. She normally does three months – March through May – and then a two month stay – October, November. She did part of her training with a professor at the university in Basle and then she worked as an intern at the clinic. They kept her on after she got her first post with the NHS over here. Then she came to us when she moved into the area with her husband's job. That's, as I said, some five years ago.

"Would you be able to say anything about the relationship? Did she seem happy to you?"

"Oh, eminently so, as far as her work is concerned. We didn't spend a great deal of time socialising. The pressure of fitting in clients doesn't leave much time for chit chat. We would have a team meeting once a month but that was focussed on any issues arising from our client group. So I can only answer your question, in that respect, very vaguely, I'm afraid. I didn't have any reason to think she was troubled by anything."

"Who were her most recent clients?"

"I'm afraid I wouldn't be in a position to disclose that; client confidentiality, you understand. If it became a matter of more serious urgency, you would need a warrant. I'm sure you're aware of that."

"Indeed so, Mrs Cavendish. So, you can't think of any reason why she would go off in this way?"

"I'm sorry I'm unable to help. I can't think of a single reason why she might disappear, or where she would be, if she didn't leave for Switzerland. Have you contacted the family? She has a sister I think I remember her saying – Lorna? Laura…? Yes, Laura's her name."

"Thank you. I know that. Let's hope we can find Mrs Innocent. I may need to come back to you about her client list."

"I understand. Let us hope, as you say, you can sort out this mystery. I'll say goodbye, Detective Inspector, and I wish you good luck with your search."

"Yes. Thank you, Mrs Cavendish. Goodbye for now. Thank you for the coffee. Oh, before I go. Did Mrs

Innocent leave her computer here at the clinic?"

"I would say no, Mr Morrison, but we'll check in the practice room she was last using. She would copy her reports, diagnoses and the like to our central hard drive, but her laptop she'd take home with her, I rather think."

They walked along the corridor together, and Mrs Cavendish stopped by and unlocked the door to a small consulting room. She invited Morrison to go in with her to look round. They checked surfaces, drawers and unlocked filing cabinets, Mrs Cavendish watching carefully to see that Morrison didn't go into any confidential files when she unlocked a storage cupboard to allow him to complete his search.

Morrison got back to the station at Belton and spotted Geoff Waller still bent over his screen at coming up to 6 p.m.

"How did you get on with the computer shop address, Geoff?"

"Hi, Sir. It turned out to be 'IT Repairs and Maintenance' at Hoywich. The owner is a chap called Ian Thompson. He wasn't in when I rang. I spoke to an assistant, Christine, his daughter, I think. She's made an arrangement for me to see him tomorrow morning. They have the laptop booked in. I'll go straight there tomorrow and pick it up and take it to ITDU."

"Good work, Geoff. I was just thinking. If you take your computer for checks on viruses, scams, stuff like that, you have to give them your access password so they can search through your files to diagnose faults. On second thoughts, bring it into the station first. If she has any of her case notes on recent clients we can read, it will give us a head start. It's a long shot but worth trying. Access is probably encrypted, but you never know. See you tomorrow, Geoff."

"Bye, Sir. There's an envelope came for you today while you were out. It might be from Dayton."

"Oh good. I was hoping we'd be hearing from him soon."

Morrison unlocked his office, hung up his jacket and worked through items left for him through the day. He left what he recognised as Dayton's envelope till last. He went to make a hot drink so that he could sit and take in the detail submitted by the pathologist. The main cause of death had been asphyxiation; blood vessel bursts in the eyes and skin of the face confirmed it. Pressure marks over nose and mouth suggested a pad had been used with a chemical cocktail to induce unconsciousness and fibres inhaled during the attack suggested something like a cushion might have been used, in addition. There was significant bruising at several points of the body and severe internal injuries caused by the instrument, Dayton hypothesised, and force used to lever the body into its hiding place in the woods. This bruising and the internal injuries had been caused after death. Nothing by way of residue in the victim's system suggested regular drug use. That plus the general health and condition of the victim suggested she was unlikely to be a sex worker. The skin of the victim was unusually pale – they'd thought when they first viewed the corpse that her skin had been painted with something, but that might have been its luminosity against the darkness of her location. Her hair colour was in the red spectrum but had been dyed over time. While smallish in stature, she would have stood out in a crowd, not only because of her natural colouring but also by being heavily breasted in relation to her slight frame recorded as five foot three inches in height. The size of the corset, Beryl had said, was 40G, but that, at the time, needn't have meant it had belonged to the victim – now perhaps it did. The victim hadn't given birth in her lifetime. There had been dental work to follow up on and records had been sought to help with identification. While no jewellery had been recovered from the body, the ring finger of the left hand indicated she had worn a ring over a lengthy period of time, suggesting she had been married. Stomach contents, which had deteriorated over the weeks the body had been undiscovered, suggested a meat-eating diet, with no evidence of alcohol having been consumed. The victim had been murdered at a place other than where she was hidden.

Morrison leafed through toxicology returns and then scrutinised the photographs. He reached into Gayle Innocent's file lying to hand and found the passport photograph her husband had given him.

It's not her then, he thought as he compared the two images. He took the photographs and affixed them to the 'Lady in the Woods' current case board. He knew instinctively that the pace of the investigation would now pick up. With that prospect he listed his action points for the next day's briefing, locked his office, shook his head as he took in again the new photographs on the board and made his way out to the car park.

Chapter 12

Edward went to the end of the short close, reversed and took in the houses either side of his approach to the Innocents' address. All seemed quiet, as before. He drove along the close and reversed into the drive, getting as close as he could to the garage but allowing for the door to lift. He selected the garage door key, fumbling a little with his gloved hands and, pulling his baseball cap down to cover his upper face, he got out of the car wearing his overalls which he'd planned would give the impression to any curious net-twitcher that he was doing a job for Mr Innocent while he himself was at work.

With the garage door opened sufficiently to give him access and a partial shield, he unloaded a toolbox on to the drive and girded himself to haul out Gayle Innocent, now sheathed in plastic and resembling a carpet. Once dumped alongside her own car in the garage, Edward then collected the toolbox, closed his boot and returned inside the garage and closed down the door. On previous visits to deposit Gayle's personal effects around the house – mobile phone, watch, rings – he'd worked out the location of the attic and the fact that it, too, had a drop-down cover with a convenient ladder attached. Less convenient was the fact that the attic space wasn't fully boarded. There were cases and removal boxes, the usual Christmas decorations, a couple of clothes rails from previous addresses, perhaps, and other unidentifiable junk. Beyond the area they occupied in the boarded area, the space narrowed into the eaves. He'd imagined how he'd position his charge in that darker recess and now he had to do it for real, carrying Gayle's dead weight and balancing across the beams.

He manoeuvred the two of them slowly, painstakingly up the confines of the steps and the grab rail and, poking through into the attic, he flopped over the edge of the boarding the top of his charge which he'd carried 'fireman fashion'. His chest burned as he forced through the opening more of the weight of his burden till he had enough balanced to free him to climb inside the attic space himself. He grabbed at the plastic and hauled in the rest, taking care not to trip as he manoeuvred through the paraphernalia stored in his way. He decided it would be safer to roll his charge across the beams into his chosen corner. With a lot of grunting and swearing, pushing and levering with his feet, he judged the body was as far into the dark corner as he could get it. He went back to the garage and took out the black sheet he'd brought with him in the toolbox and returned to the attic to cover the plastic-wrapped corpse of Gayle Innocent, once more resident at her home address. He rearranged the cases and boxes slightly to mask the access to the corner he'd chosen, checked and double checked that what he'd delivered wouldn't be immediately obvious. He looked at the time and saw that he'd spent longer than intended. He reversed his route through the house, checking behind him that nothing obvious was left of his visit, locked all the doors that he'd unlocked, picked up his toolbox, opened and re-closed the garage door and, having put his toolbox back in his boot, he started up and cruised slowly through the close and back on to the main road.

He felt slightly sorry. The body was safely lodged in its

intended resting place, but it was now over to other circumstances for it to be found and Philip Innocent named as the culprit. He drove home thinking about how he could bring that about.

Chapter 13

Philip called Laura. She answered straight away.

"Philip? How are you? Any news?"

"Hi Laura. That's why I'm ringing. Morrison has been on the phone. That number for the computer repair shop turned out to be a local repair and maintenance place. The police worked out the address and contacted them. Gayle's laptop had been booked in for a software upgrade. She was to pick it up on the fifteenth. That was the missed message. They collected it but couldn't access anything of any use, so have sent it off to their IT diagnostic unit to see if they can unlock it."

"Well, that's progress."

"Yes, but I'm still confused. Why was she making me think she was leaving on the fourteenth when her flight was booked for the seventeenth? Where is she? If she has another phone, I've no number for it and she's not contacting me. Morrison wants the phone I found in the lounge. I'm taking it in tomorrow before work."

"We can have some hope that they'll find something that isn't obvious to you and me. Have you got a list of her numbers and who the people are?"

"I made a file of them and started calling some of the ones that I didn't recognise, but it's a slow business getting people in at home and answering or getting them to call you back if you leave a voicemail. I'm not so sure about ringing her friends. It seems strange, asking if they know where my own wife is. Has she contacted you?"

"No, absolutely not. Was there any indication she was unhappy?"

"Not that I was aware. I said when I first rang you that she was a bit standoffish but I didn't think it was anything other than women's stuff or pressure at work before she was due in Basle, and we were going to be together meeting up the following weekend anyway. So I'm stumped to come up with a reason for all this. In fact, I'm beginning to think something really has happened to her. We're used to being apart while she's working away but we've always been in contact. I mean, it's the end of March this week. I can't ring her, and she's not ringing me. What am I going to do? I can't concentrate on my work. I'm lost here at home. Police checks take time and they've got the pressure of another case at the moment."

"Do they know who that is?"

"No, well, they're not saying, if they do. There's nothing in the local press yet, at any rate. Morrison did confirm to me it wasn't Gayle. I'd given him a passport photo of Gayle when I went in to report her missing... and it couldn't ever have been Gayle, really. I dropped her at the airport the same afternoon that I checked one of the lower walkways at Birkacre Woods where I found the body... Oh, blast. I shouldn't have told you that. Don't say anything to anyone."

"Whaat? You found a body?"

"Yes, and reported it to the police but I'm not supposed to say anything about it – so don't you either. The certainty that matters for us is that it isn't Gayle."

"Well, thanks be to God for that."

After talking to Laura for another few minutes, he finished their call by promising to keep her posted on any developments. He went into the study to look up something for work and saw a watch in one of the drawers he was sifting through for a folder. He couldn't remember it being here before and picked it up to examine it more closely. It was Gayle's. He'd bought it for her some years ago. Had she left it behind and taken another one? He tried to recall what she'd been wearing when he gave her the lift to the airport. He could tick off a mental list of jacket, trousers, shoes and case but he had not an iota of memory of what she might have been wearing as a watch.

He went upstairs to their bedroom and hunted for Gayle's small jewellery case. It wasn't there but, then again, it wouldn't be. She'd have taken it with her in her luggage. As he tried to reassure himself that she'd probably been wearing another watch, something more dressy maybe for Switzerland, he caught his breath as his eye noticed her rings nestled in among some underwear. He couldn't believe his eyes. He was certain she'd been wearing them when they'd exchanged goodbyes. Was he kidding himself? He hadn't noticed her watch. Why did he think he'd seen her with her rings on? Did she always leave her stuff behind when she went to Basle? He'd never thought to consider it before. He couldn't say. He felt confused and angry with himself that he didn't know. What else might he not know? He determined to mention his finds to Morrison when he took Gayle's phone into the station.

He rang ahead to his office to say he would be at the station before going on to see someone about the new project. He advised calling Councillor Stevens to await his call when he was finished with Morrison. He parked and walked to the entrance, recalling the first time he'd come to report his find in Birkacre Woods. Waiting once more, while his request to see Morrison was relayed through the door in the wall, his eyes roamed across the various notices posted amid the clutter of faded advisory helplines and information sheets. His gaze became fixed as he swallowed hard, seeing the face staring out at him from a newish 'Do you know this woman?' poster. He was about to approach closer when Morrison came through the door behind the counter, lifted the flap and invited him to come through. They entered one of the interview rooms and sat opposite each other, as before.

"You were bringing in your wife's mobile phone, Mr Innocent?"

"Yes. I've got it with me. I made a file of the contact numbers and I'd started to ring round some of the ones I didn't recognise. I've printed out some notes of who people were, who answered my calls or called back at a later date, but the list is far from complete."

"Tell me where you found it."

"I got home from my visit to Birkacre Woods where I found the body that I reported to you the following day. It was quite late in the evening by then, and I just sat down in the lounge to watch a bit of news and felt the thing down in the chair. I thought it was the remote, but it turned out to be this phone. I put it on charge to find out whose it was, since I'd seen Gayle phoning on her mobile after I'd dropped her off at the airport."

"So, let's see… that was the afternoon of the fourteenth."

"Absolutely correct. I came in to speak to you the next day… and," he rummaged in his pocket and drew out the watch and jewellery he'd found around the house, "there's this as well."

He set the watch and rings on the desk in front of Morrison.

"What are these, Mr Innocent?"

"They're my wife's watch and rings. I came across the watch when I was looking for a folder for work. It was in one of the drawers in our study. I went to look in Gayle's drawers in our bedroom for her small jewellery case and, as I was telling myself she'd have it with her in her suitcase, I came across her rings in among her things in her underwear drawer."

"Did she usually leave her jewellery behind when she travelled?"

"That's what I've been asking myself over and over. It's possible she chose another watch to wear in Switzerland. I bought her this one. She did have another one for dressy occasions, but I can't for the life of me remember what she was wearing on her wrist when I gave her a lift. I thought she would be wearing her rings but I can't just remember. I can't picture her hands."

"We'll bag these up, Mr Innocent, if that's ok with you?"

"Of course. Has anything come in yet about the laptop?"

"Not, as yet. It will take time to unlock your wife's system for keeping her professional records confidential. We had access to her system via Mr Thomas, the IT maintenance chappie, but we couldn't make any progress beyond that. It's with our diagnostic unit, as we speak. Well be in touch when we have anything further to report. I take it your wife hasn't been in contact?"

"No. I've been keeping in touch with her sister, Laura. She hasn't heard anything from Gayle either. I must admit that I've been reluctant to contact her friends. It's difficult to ask them if they've heard from my own wife, you know."

"Leave that to us then."

Morrison rose, suggesting that the interview was over. He led Philip back to the reception area and, as he was dropping the counter flap into place and saying goodbye, Philip stopped at the poster of the missing woman and said, "You know, this has the look of a woman I did some work with."

"Who would that be, Mr Innocent?"

"It wouldn't be her. I was just saying that there's a resemblance. This woman has close-cropped hair."

"That's because her hair has been shaved. What's the name of the woman you think our lady resembles? We've issued the poster to get some help with ID."

Philip was beginning to wish he had never spoken.

"Oh, I don't really think it could be Margaret. I don't want the police going round, saying I've given her name."

"I'm sure she would understand that we were asking for the public's help to identify what, after all, Mr Innocent, was the body you yourself found and reported to us."

Philip's mouth opened and closed.

"Come back through and we'll take some details. I assure you, Mr Innocent, we will deal confidentially with any information you give us. Any help you can give us would be most useful, even if only to eliminate this lady from our enquiries. We're hoping for more people like you, coming and saying or calling us to say who it might be. We check out any information we're given as unobtrusively as data protection allows."

With some reluctance, Philip returned to the interview room. Morrison retrieved a pad from one of the desk drawers.

"Now, Mr Innocent. What is the name of this woman?"

"Margaret Culpebble. Mrs – she's married. Her husband is called Edward."

"Do you know where she lives?"

"Not exactly, but she lived out in Botswortham somewhere. When I worked with her, she was a civil servant at the DEFRA offices in Stenport."

"How did your paths cross?"

"I had to gather evidence for a report to Government Office in Sheffield, compiling returns from the foot-and-mouth outbreak we had in the North a bit back. She was one of the team that helped collate all the findings from meetings with council groups, agricultural associations – all kinds of groups and individuals affected. The offices at Stenport will be able to give you contact details. I left the Agency some time ago for the firm I work with now – EnviroOptions in Reychol.

"Well, thank you, Mr Innocent. Rest assured that we'll treat your information with great care and, as you say, it will hopefully turn out not to be our lady in the woods."

For the second time, Morrison led Philip out through the door in the wall to the station's reception area.

Morrison returned to the main office and looked for someone from his team to follow up on Philip's details. Beryl was sifting through lists when he put his head round the door.

"Beryl, just the one! What are you dealing with at the minute?"

"I'm still working through these underwear retailers. I've a couple of local addresses to follow up on in the Arcade shopping complex."

"Good. That's near enough to Stenport for me. Take these details and check with HQ –speak to CI Stanford – for the go-ahead to check the DEFRA employee database. It's a suggestion for the ID of our lady in the woods. It's time we were getting to know her better and, more to the point, why she ended up there."

"Ok Sir. Which do you want me to do first?"

"Try HQ first. If we get some luck straight away, it will make things easier for your follow-up enquiries. Here, take this!"

Morrison handed over a copy of the notes he'd taken about Margaret Culpebble. It was an unusual name and would soon show up, if she were still a current DEFRA employee.

"Don't forget to take a poster pic with you, just in case there's more than one Margaret Culpebble. If it comes up, tell the person dealing with you that her hair had been shaved off. It was red to start with and then dyed."

"If I get an ok today, do you want me to go over to the DEFRA offices?"

"It's unlikely you'll get it today but, yes, if wonders never cease. See, if you can get a current photo. They'll be curious. We don't want anything getting out to the press yet. I'm surprised nobody's been round here sniffing since we put the posters out."

"Ok Sir. See you later or tomorrow. I'd like to check these two retailers in the Arcade. It would be two from a long list that I've got."

"Sure. Phone, text, message me if you get anything from DEFRA. I could nip out to the address this afternoon if we've anything to go on."

Philip turned into his drive and switched off the car's engine. He sat for a moment, thinking about the twists and turns of the day. That poster had spooked him. He wished he had never spoken to Morrison about it. He hoped for himself and Margaret that the resemblance he'd spotted would turn out to be just that. It was strange, too, about the head being shaved. He remembered his reaction when the corset had been spotted by Morrison and the reference to the whiteness of the victim's skin. That could be explained by the effect of the darkness of their environment, throwing everything lighter into relief, but he'd instantly thought of Margaret.

He opened his front door and bent to pick up the day's post. One corner sported a smiling sun and a travel company logo. More junk, he thought. He dropped his case in the study and prepared his evening meal. He turned on the radio to catch the day's news, laying his place setting and condiments. While waiting for the microwave to ping on his ready meal, he sifted through the post. Finishing the last of his sweet and sour chicken, he wiped his mouth and fingers with the tear-off sheet from the kitchen roll and opened his last two envelopes. One was his invoice for electricity and the other he was about to bin unopened when he saw that it was addressed to him. He tore open the envelope and read the details about air travel to Australia at Business Class rates – six thousand pounds. He read through the information again, more carefully. It wasn't a promotion. It was an actual flight arranged for him, he noticed, coinciding with his birthday. Payment had been made by card. The last four digits he didn't recognise as from his own card and he wondered with an excited glimmer of hope that it was from Gayle's card. He checked the date of the transaction – 22nd March, the day after his return from Basle. His thoughts and emotions raced inside his head and chest. What was this about? Where was Gayle? Was this some surprise gift and she would suddenly appear in some smiling 'reveal'?

He phoned Laura but had to leave a message.

He rang Morrison who answered and listened to his excited presentation of this indication that Gayle was alive somewhere. Morrison punctured his momentary high.

"Is this the kind of thing that has happened before? Does it match your wife's personality? Is it in character?"

"Well, no, now that you ask, but it's surely a sign that

she's around somewhere?"

"Is there any indication how the ticket was arranged? If it was done online we could get the folk at ITDU to check her computer. Have you a date for when it was arranged?"

"March twenty-second."

"Well. It won't be via her computer then, unless Mr Thomas is buying you air travel which is unlikely. Can you bring in the paperwork for us to check through? If it's been done in a travel agent's or over the phone, we can chase that up. I take it that you won't be making the flight?"

Feeling punctured and deflated, Philip answered that he would want the trip cancelled and that he would drop the paperwork at the station before work the next day.

Chapter 14

The first weeks of April saw the buzz of activity in the main office pick up pace. Morrison had portioned out the longer list of tasks and searches required, following the focus being made more local. The clutch of coincidences had led to the Lady in the Woods having been identified as Mrs Margaret Culpebble, a DEFRA employee working out of the offices at Stenport. Beryl Gillibrand had been given confirmation that the large-breasted size corset had, indeed, been purchased from one of the shops in the Arcade complex. Further contacts with the credit card company had identified a Mrs M Culpebble as the purchaser the previous year when the shop had been holding a sale. The sales assistant had remembered the item because it had taken so long to sell. It was of a size that not many people could have hoped to fit into.

The contact details from DEFRA, when finally presented, didn't lead to a similar quick conclusion to that part of the case. Morrison had called at the address with Andrew Raby in tow, but no-one had answered the door. Checks with the few neighbours in the small, well-spaced development didn't provide much useful information beyond the usual scenario of the couple keeping themselves to themselves; though one pensioner lady, who was able to identify the DEFRA picture as being Mrs Culpebble, was unable to say when she had last seen her. The pensioner's husband, a Mr Nelson, had told them that Mr Culpebble owned a small refrigeration plant nearby. He couldn't say where, or if, he was currently working. He might have been away, since they hadn't seen his BMW car around. Mr Culpebble had been burning leaves in the back garden but that had been some weeks before. He was able to remember because it had happened twice: the first time in February and then again in March. Having thanked Mr and Mrs Nelson and left them a number to contact when Mr Culpebble returned, the two CID officers made their way back to the Culpebble property. They couldn't see much of the rear garden, which was bordered by leylandii screening, because the side gate to the rear garden was secured.

Morrison instructed Raby to check local industrial developments, Chambers of Commerce and Companies House to get an address and ownership of any refrigeration plants within twenty miles. Until they could speak to Mr Culpebble at his home address, they would try and pin him down at his business address.

Back at the office Morrison set a progress meeting for later that afternoon.

Edward had no sooner lugged his case upstairs than the doorbell rang. He looked out of his bedroom window but couldn't see anyone, or a vehicle to identify the caller. The bell rang again. He went downstairs, trying to gauge, by the shadow in the side panel, who it might be standing before the door. He opened it onto the face of one of his neighbours.

"Mr Nelson, what can I do for you?"

"Hello, Mr Culpebble. You're back I see. Have you been away?"

"I have, yes. What can I do for you?"

"A few days ago we had a visit by two police officers. They were looking for you and were asking questions about your wife. Did we recognise her photo? Did we know where she was? When had we last seen her? Where did you work? Things like that."

"I see. Did they say why they were asking all these questions?"

"They gave us a number to contact when we saw you back again. My wife said I should give you a chance to ring them yourself before she did."

Edward wondered whether the comment suggested a genuine act of kindness or a threat.

"That was thoughtful of her. Will you thank her for me? Have you the number? I'll give them a call straight away. I wonder why they were asking about Margaret."

"My wife and I were saying that we haven't seen her around for a while. Is everything all right?"

"I'm sorry to tell you and your wife, Mr Nelson, but people will soon find out, I suppose, that things didn't work out between us. My wife has left me."

"Oh, I'm so sorry. Excuse me."

"That's alright. To be honest with you, it's a relief. I was under a lot of pressure with my business and arguments on top of all that were making life unbearable."

Edward looked sad as, first, Mr Nelson reached out to squeeze his arm gently and, then, to pat it consolingly.

"Have you the number with you, Mr Nelson?"

"Oh, yes. Here you are. I've written it down."

"Thank you and don't forget to thank Mrs Nelson."

"Yes, I will. If there's anything we can do to be of help, just call. We are in most of the time."

"I'll bear that in mind, Mr Nelson. Goodbye."

With that, Edward drew the paper from Mr Nelson's hand and closed the door. He congratulated himself on keeping his temper when he was inwardly seething. He wondered whether Margaret had been found, or if someone from DEFRA had raised a query at her not appearing for work. While he had his story worked out for the latter, he had not expected her body to be found this soon. He weighed up whether Mrs Nelson would have rung the number before sending her husband across to speak to him. He decided to leave calling till later when he'd unpacked and had something to eat. He would work out a story by then.

Morrison heard from his team what material had been gathered, what searches were still ongoing and what would have to be instigated following new information.

Beryl had confirmed Philip Innocent's suggestion that the name of their Lady in the Woods was Margaret Culpebble, mid-forties, employee of DEFRA at Stenport, married twenty years to a man, Edward Culpebble, ten years her senior. She gave additional confirmation that Margaret Culpebble had purchased the Beaulieu corset in which her dead body had been dressed. DEFRA human resources finally came up with her attendance record following her application by letter for leave of absence on compassionate grounds: the death of her mother. She hadn't yet been recorded as resuming her employment. Morrison briefed them about his and Andy's visit to the address supplied by DEFRA. Mr Culpebble hadn't been available for questioning. Neighbours, Mr and Mrs Nelson, had suggested that Edward Culpebble was the owner of a refrigeration plant somewhere nearby, which Andy was following up on. The Nelsons had been given a contact number for whenever they saw that Mr Culpebble had returned. Andrew Raby set out the details about three of the four refrigeration plants listed in the area.

He was still waiting to hear from the last, based in Buxby Bridge. He'd been to the address for it on a small industrial estate but hadn't been able to get near the offices. The gate in the perimeter fence had been padlocked. He'd asked around other units on the site without gaining any information about the owner of the plant. He was currently awaiting news from the leaseholder of the site as to the person's ID.

"Good. Keep at it, Andrew. Mr Nelson seemed to have his wits about him when we were speaking to him. We'll know for certain when we hear from the site owner. Now, Geoff. Where are you up to with Gayle Innocent's laptop?"

Geoff Waller told them that ITDU had produced a list of clients from the period since her return from Switzerland last November through to her most recent client. The only details were initials, number and dates of appointments and a reference number. With nothing much to go on, they would have to access the clinic's files. Morrison told Geoff to get a warrant from Brian Bickerstaffe and to make an appointment with Mrs Cavendish at the clinic when he had one. They would go and see her together.

For the remainder of their meeting they gave updates on bailings, court cases pending and ongoing, and news of releases from prison that put ex-cons back on their patch.

On Thursday afternoon the phone rang in Morrison's office.

"Yes, Mrs Nelson. This is Detective Inspector Morrison speaking. Go ahead... I see. Thank you for letting me know."

Morrison returned to the group of staff working at

their respective terminals.

"Andrew, leave what you're doing. Mrs Nelson's just been on the phone. Mr Culpebble's turned up. Let's get over there before he disappears somewhere else."

Morrison stopped at the end of Mr Culpebble's drive. The BMW was parked at the front of the house. They looked for signs of occupation but detected no movement.

"Ok, Andy. Let's see what Mr Culpebble has to say."

The two approached the front door and rang the bell. Edward, working in his downstairs study at the back of the house, found a window on the front to see who might be calling. He saw the car parked at the end of his drive. He opened the door as the shorter of the two men pulled out a wallet from his pocket and opened it for Mr Culpebble to check.

"Detective Inspector Morrison from Belton Police. This is my colleague Detective Sergeant Raby. May we come in? It is Mr Culpebble, yes?"

"I'm Edward Culpebble. That's correct. Come in. How can I help you?"

"We would like to ask you some questions about your wife, Margaret Culpebble."

"I see. Come this way."

Edward showed them into the lounge.

"Mr Nelson came across when I'd just got back the other day, saying you'd been on our estate asking questions. What is this about?"

"Did he tell you that we'd left a contact number?"

"No. Should he have done?"

"We were trying to locate you through your business address. Mr Nelson told us that you worked at a refrigeration plant in the area."

"That was the case, Mr Morrison, but I sold it some time ago. The new owner is a Mr Scott. Mark Scott."

"My colleague contacted all the refrigeration plants in the area and across the county boundary, but we couldn't find a trace."

"I can't think why not. It's on the industrial unit site in Buxby Bridge."

"My colleague went to visit that address but it was all closed up."

"Perhaps Mark Scott is delaying his installation. Problems with the bank, maybe. He's opening an engineering unit. I can't explain why he's not yet in business there."

"About your wife, Mr Culpebble. Your neighbours say they haven't seen her for some time. May we ask why?"

"Like I said to Mr Nelson, it didn't work out between us. She left me. I was under a lot of pressure with my business. There were lots of arguments. She told me she had met someone who had more time for her and made her feel more of a woman than I had done for some time. I have to say, when she packed up her things and left, it was a bit of a relief.

"Do you know who the person is that she left you for?"

"Some bloke she worked with at DEFRA in Stenport."

"Have you heard from your wife since?"

"She hasn't rung me here but she contacted me at my business, saying she was taking time off to get her head together. She was going to call me later with details of where I could get in contact with her for things like post or solicitor's letters. I've tried ringing her mobile but get no answer, suggesting she's maybe changed her phone or got herself a new number. I've drawn a blank with people at DEFRA who say she's not back from leave and, of course, I haven't any forwarding address from her for you to go and speak to her yourselves.

"It sounds like she was trying to make a complete break. I'm sorry to have to ask you again about the person she was involved with, but have you any clue as to that person's identity, or where he… it is a he, I presume… can be contacted? It's important, Mr Culpebble."

"Margaret was visiting places across the North following the last outbreak of foot-and-mouth. I rang her one evening and couldn't get through at the hotel she said she was staying at. I rang again early the next morning and was put through to her room. I heard a man's voice which my wife passed off as belonging to a colleague of hers – Muriel Turnbill from Environmental Services. It's just unfortunate that I'd run into Muriel the evening before when I was shopping in town at the supermarket. I knew Margaret was lying to me. So, whoever he is, he'll be one of the team who went to Blakethwaite in Cumbria. It was the Deer Horn Inn."

Edward gave Raby the details, going away to check for any phone number he might have.

"I wonder why he said he didn't have our contact number, Sir?"

"I was thinking exactly the same. Mrs Nelson told me her husband had written it on a piece of paper for him. We'll not mention it for the moment. You'll need to check with staff at the hotel in Blakethwaite and get names of all the DEFRA group staying at the hotel. We need to find out who she's meant to have gone off with. Sh! Mr C is coming back."

"I can't find it. I've no record of it on my mobile either. I must have deleted it. I'm sorry I can't be of any help."

"That's fine. Thanks anyway. Don't bother about it

now. Come and sit down. I have something to tell you."

"Is it Margaret? Has she been in an accident? Oh God, no!"

"Please sit down, Mr Culpebble… We have found a woman's body and are trying to identify it. We put posters up asking for the public's help. You haven't seen any?"

"No. I've been away. Do you mean it might not be Margaret? What's happened? Tell me, Inspector!"

"We received a tip-off from a member of the public suggesting a resemblance between the woman in our poster and your wife. Andy, have you the copy with you?"

Andy reached into his folder for the poster and passed it across to Edward. He studied the face in the picture for some time.

"It certainly does bear a strong resemblance to Margaret, but this woman has close-cropped hair. Margaret's hair is a lot longer."

"Are you saying this is not your wife, Mr Culpebble?"

"Yes… no… I'm not absolutely certain. It certainly looks like her… but the hair…"

"I wonder, Mr Culpebble, if you would be willing to come with us and tell us finally, if this person is or isn't your wife?"

"What? Now?"

"No. I'll arrange something with Dr Dayton, the pathologist, get back in touch with you and arrange a time."

"As soon as possible, eh? I don't want it hanging over me that this woman may be Margaret, if it isn't."

"I understand, Mr Culpebble. It will probably be tomorrow morning. Will that be convenient?"

"Of course. I'll wait to hear from you, Inspector.

Anything else?"

"No, not for the moment."

Morrison and Raby left the house having exchanged contact numbers with Edward, with every hope that a session would be organised with Dr Dayton for the next morning.

"So, what did you make of all that, Andrew?"

The two of them sat in the car at the end of Edward's drive, comparing mental notes.

"My question remains about why he didn't contact us, if he had been given the number by Mr Nelson. He seems plausible in other things that he said. We need to check out the story about her meeting someone on the DEFRA team. I'll check with staff at the Deer Horn Inn for names of personnel and get them to check their phone records to see if he did call, as he said he did. Muriel Turnbill should be easy enough to find to corroborate his story about meeting her in the supermarket."

"My thinking entirely. I'll take Geoff down to Gayle Innocent's clinic. We can check the detail of her case files and, while I'm debriefing Philip Innocent, I'll ask him if he knows who Margaret Culpebble was cosying up to."

"It couldn't be him, Sir?"

"Well, as they say in these matters, we're not counting anything out. I'd think, though, he'd have enough on his plate, working out where and why his wife has gone AWOL, but we'll hear what he has to say. See what you can pull together. We'll check progress tomorrow afternoon. Brief the team. Make it for 6 p.m."

Chapter 15

Later that same day Morrison and Geoff Waller walked up to the clinic reception. The receptionist asked for their appointment details and walked them through to see Mrs Cavendish after she'd finished with her client.

"Hello again, Inspector Morrison. You've come to look through Doctor Innocent's case notes, I believe."

"Indeed Mrs Cavendish. We've accessed Dr Innocent's laptop but have only initials, date information and reference numbers. My colleague here, Detective Constable Waller, will show you our credentials."

Geoff Waller unfolded and passed across to Mrs Cavendish the warrant authorisation to search and read the relevant files from between the quoted dates.

"I'm hoping we don't have to search further back than Dr Innocent's return from her November stint in Switzerland through to the last sighting of her on the fourteenth of March this year. If we can't find anything helpful with that batch of files, my colleague, Constable Waller, will seek out a new authorisation to dig deeper."

"Your authorisation is to read in situ. I can't allow the files to leave the premises, I'm afraid. Client confidentiality is paramount, particularly in our specialist field. If anything is later required as evidence, then we'll expect the lawyer's subpoena."

"Exactly so, Mrs Cavendish. Perhaps you'll allow us access to the file storage office."

Mrs Cavendish led the two men along the corridor to the office Morrison had searched through on his first visit. She opened the door and unlocked the storage cupboard, lifting out the relevant batch of files. She'd obviously prepared ahead for their visit.

"I'll see to it that you're undisturbed while you do what you have to do."

Mrs Cavendish locked the file cupboard and asked them to check with Miss Lester, the receptionist, for any help they might need in the interim.

Morrison and Geoff Waller took off their jackets and set to work at the table provided.

"What are we looking for, Sir? Anything in particular?"

"Where's the list of dates and initials you got from ITDU, Geoff?"

Geoff Waller laid the sheet on the table between them. Morrison divided the pile of folders and told Geoff to match initials and dates to full contact details on the files, writing a brief note about the contents to differentiate their reasons for attendance at the clinic. After an hour Geoff got up to stretch his legs and asked his boss if he wanted a drink. He made his way back to the reception counter and chatted with Miss Lester.

"What's the 'B' for, if you don't mind me asking?"

"Barbara, but in the family I'm called Bowie."

"Why's that?"

"It was my brother…"

"Don't tell me he was a David Bowie fan?"

"No, not really. My older brother couldn't get his tongue and teeth round Barbara after I was christened. Bowie kind of stuck."

"Any chance of some coffee… Bowie? Please? Is it alright to call you Bowie?"

"Be my guest. I'll bring your coffee down to you. Where are you…? Ok, the file room it is."

Geoff winked at her and made his way back along the corridor.

"Chatting up the staff, Geoff?"

Geoff smiled and resumed the sift through the folders.

After another hour had elapsed, Morrison drained the last of his coffee and suggested they compare findings.

"Most of mine are females, Sir, general reason for attending – STD infections. I've one bloke, a Mr Rowan McCord, 50s, recent referral. He last saw Dr Innocent on the twelfth, am appointment. Sexually inactive, but there's nothing written up for the last session. I've an address but no telephone number.

"Is he married?"

"It says twenty years, Sir."

"I'm concentrating on male clients out of my pile. If she's run off with anyone, a first assumption would suggest male, till we check out all the males first. All of this might be barking up the wrong tree, obviously, but we have to check everything until we draw a blank or the lady in question comes back home. My males are James Richardson, twenty-nine, single: counselling for transgender issues, address in Stoccelten but no phone number. Then there's Hector Sidebotham, sixty-three, lives in Landley, divorced. Has a new partner, somewhat younger than him – Julie; problems with premature ejaculation.

"Poor sod. All that new action and he's not up to it."

"It's not always hunky dory with you young bucks, so don't be too quick to poke fun. At least he's recognised he's got a problem and is trying to do something about it."

"Ok, Sir. I'll just take this tray back up to reception."

"Make sure you've got all the contact details copied before you do that. We don't want you getting all doe-eyed with the receptionist and forgetting what we've spent these last hours working on. I'm ready for a sandwich myself. I'll let Mrs C know we've finished for this visit, then we'll start some checks on our three male clients."

Back at the station the team gathered for their regular check on cases in progress. Morrison came out of his office and acknowledged each of his team. Fresh back from his visit with Geoff to the clinic, he had rung Dayton, the pathologist, to arrange a viewing of the body of Margaret Culpebble, as it was believed to be. Dayton had been able to confirm a possible match, having received dental records that he had begun checking through. Morrison arranged a morning viewing and called Edward Culpebble to give him details of the arrangement. He brought his staff up to date with that event for the following morning and how he and Geoff had been occupied at the clinic on the Gayle Innocent case. Following on from their first visit to Edward Culpebble's address, Andy had contacted Deer Horn Inn and was waiting for details of DEFRA personnel overnighting in the twenty-four hour period in which Edward Culpebble had supposedly phoned and for confirmation either way that the calls had been made.

The question that remained hanging in the air was why Culpebble hadn't rung them at the station when the neighbour called round to give him the contact number after their first visit to the estate. Morrison added that they might raise that with him when he came for the next day's viewing over at Forensics.

"Do you suspect him, Sir?"

"Well, you know, Beryl, at this stage of the investigation, everything is a possibility. His wife has left him. He talked about relief when she'd taken her things and walked out. Being the husband, he's as much a suspect as anybody. Whether we build a case with him as the focus, depends on what we pursue from the Deer Horn Inn's records. He was under pressure with his business, though we haven't yet asked what the reason for that was. Did he lash out when he got wind that his wife was playing away? Is all that a fabrication anyway? Beryl, what did DEFRA state as the reason for Mrs Culpebble's application for LOA?"

"The death of her mother."

"Did that check out?"

"I was just going to add that records show her mother died five years ago."

"It looks like we have to unravel what the truth to that is and who's telling it. Another question for Mr Culpebble tomorrow. He stated to Andy and myself that she had gone off to get her head together."

"She could have invented that to get time off to go flat or house-hunting, if something wasn't already set up with this lover-boy."

"Right on, Geoff. It's all speculation at this stage. Ok Geoff, while you're at it, tell us all, if you've found anything for us since earlier this afternoon."

"A bit of a poser on my list to follow up on. I have a Rowan McCord to interview. He was one of the last clients on Gayle Innocent's appointments' listing before she supposedly disappeared. The address for him turns out to be a multi-occupancy address, mostly students, in Stenport

North. I was out there just and managed to talk to two tenants – Julie Philbin, doing an accountancy course, and Kishan Sinha, a second year engineering student. Julie laughed when I gave her the age of Rowan McCord. She said that, while there were all kinds passing through the place, someone in their fifties would have stood out like a sore thumb, since he definitely wasn't the owner. She gave me contact details for the landlord, and he later confirmed to me that no-one called Rowan McCord had ever lived at the address, nor, as far as he knew, had ever undertaken any repair or maintenance work on the property. He was going to double-check with the firms he normally uses and get back to me. Mr Sinha answered in much the same way that Miss Philbin had. He's been at the address since he started his course and hasn't known anyone of McCord's name to have been a resident or involved with the property.

"McCord's obviously disguising his identity then."

"It's a possibility, Beryl, considering the nature of the therapy at the clinic. The address is looking like it's false. I have some more checking to do before I'm able to say whether his name is a false one. Then we will be up against it. They don't keep photo ID of the clients at the clinic."

Morrison gave Geoff his checklist from the clinic to be working on while he and Andy met Edward Culpebble the next day. Beryl was to pick up the Deer Horn Inn data, if it came through while he and Andy were over at Dayton's offices.

Chapter 16

Edward had wondered what approach to take when confronted with his wife's corpse. He'd wavered about an immediate recognition when the policeman had shown him the poster. He didn't think he could repeat and get away with a similar performance. He decided to identify her positively – the mole between her shoulder blades would clinch it – and then he would show an emotional reaction. He knew he wouldn't be dealing with fools, so he would have to be on his guard.

Morrison and the colleague, who had accompanied him on their visit to his address, were waiting to greet him when he arrived at the reception counter.

"Thank you for coming so promptly, Mr Culpebble. This, you may remember from last time, is my colleague DS Raby."

The two men nodded their recognition.

"We are going to take you to the room where people view someone who has recently died and been brought here for a post-mortem. We'll leave you on your own for a while to decide if it's your wife or not. The pathologist's assistant will be on hand in the small office adjoining.

Morrison opened the door to allow Edward through to where the body was laid out on a trolley. The assistant, who was drawing back the sheet as Edward moved into the room, withdrew into the office. Edward approached the body, conscious that he might be being studied from some vantage point he couldn't discern. He winced involuntarily when he took in his handiwork. Such parts of Margaret's dead body that he could see were horribly bruised. In using the iron fence stake to lever and push her body into the space among the tree roots, he hadn't been thinking about the after-effects. The rise in the sheet over the top half of her body reminded him of her overlarge breasts that he had come to disdain. He moved around the top half of her body. The shaved head effect he'd seen in the poster was muted by the tiny halo of hair which had sprouted after death. The cuts left in her scalp, after he'd shaved her hair, he could still make out. He called out to the pathologist's assistant.

"Can you check for me if there's a mole between her shoulder blades, please?"

The assistant pulled on rubber gloves and raised and turned the body for Edward to check. In among the bruising over her upper back he couldn't spot the mole so easily and bent nearer to peer.

Morrison and Raby, watching from above, speculated on what he might be doing but didn't move to interrupt the viewing.

"My wife had a mole between her shoulder blades but I can't see it in among all that discolouration. Did you find one?"

The assistant flashed up images on the terminal screen and enlarged the one showing her upper back to pinpoint the mole. He used a digital highlighter to circle the location of the mole on the corpse's back.

"Ah, yes. That's it. I can see it now."

At that point Edward slumped into a chair near the door, and anyone watching would have seen his shoulders heave before his hand rose to cover his face. He rocked slightly on the chair. DS Raby came into the room.

"Detective Inspector Morrison would like to speak to you, Mr Culpebble. Can you come with me?"

Raby helped Edward to his feet and, supporting him at his elbow, led him through a short corridor to an office where Morrison was waiting. Morrison pulled out a chair for Edward.

"Have a seat, Mr Culpebble…"

Morrison waited while Edward settled himself. He seemed genuinely shocked.

"I'm sorry, Mr Culpebble. I take it from your reaction that the victim is your wife, Margaret?"

"Who would do such a thing? My wife might have left me, but I would in no way wish her ill. That in there… I can't think why anyone would hate a person so much they would… ugh… they must be sick in the head."

Morrison let him vent his shock.

"Once again, Mr Culpebble, I'm sorry to have to ask you to confirm whether the body you've seen is your wife, Margaret?"

Edward's hands wiped his forehead and eyes before he looked into Morrison's face.

"It is my wife, Detective Inspector. Have you found the man who's done this to her? The bastard!"

"I can assure you, Mr Culpebble, that we are making extensive enquiries. We are following up on the details you gave us yesterday morning, and, now that you have officially confirmed that the body is your ex-wife, we will be able to focus our resources more effectively. I'm afraid that I won't be able to spare you the intrusion of such enquiries. We will need to look over your house as her last known address."

"But she took everything with her, Inspector."

"It will just be myself and DS Raby in the first instance. We are now dealing with a murder enquiry which has a confirmed victim ID, thanks to your visit this morning. We have to make checks to eliminate people or deal with them as suspects. You being the husband, and your wife having left you without trace, as it has turned out, we must try and eliminate you first and foremost. I hope you can see that, Mr Culpebble."

"Yes, obviously. When will you come, then I can arrange to be in?"

"Oh, we'll follow you down, Mr Culpebble. Sergeant Raby will drive back with you while I sort out some things with Doctor Dayton's staff. I shall be with you shortly."

Morrison and Raby spent the rest of the morning working methodically through the rooms at Edward's address, checking contents of cupboards and drawers while Edward stayed in his study. He, for his part, checked and rechecked his memory for having removed anything directly relating to Gayle Innocent from the case he had stored in his attic. The rest of her disposable stuff in the garage he had burned earlier in the year along with Margaret's bits and pieces. He calculated that there wasn't a significant difference between the sizes of the two women that would raise questions among two men making a cursory search through the case. He was behind the game in terms of how quickly the body had been found. Still, he felt his tracks had been sufficiently well covered beyond that.

Raby knocked sharply at his study door and came in even as he was concluding this.

"DI Morrison would like you to show us the attic space, Mr Culpebble."

"Certainly. Anything to help."

Edward made the attic space accessible to the two men and stood back while they climbed inside. He mounted the wooden steps and watched as the two men sifted through the myriad stuff stored there.

"I hope it's easier for you with the floor boarded, Inspector."

"That's alright, Mr Culpebble, we'll manage from here. What's the case at the end?"

"I'm not exactly sure. Maybe it's bits and pieces Margaret stored away that she no longer used. It's not mine. I'm certain of that."

"I thought you said she took everything with her?"

"I rather thought she had. I haven't been up here in a while. It didn't occur to me to check. With all the stuff she packed into the taxi, I thought she'd cleared everything out. She left some shoes. They weren't of interest to me, so I took them down to a charity shop a bit since."

"Ok, Mr Culpebble. I'm coming down. See, Andy, if there's anything else up here while I do the study and we'll look over the garage, as well."

Down in the study Morrison worked his way through the filing cabinet and drawers of the desk. In seeing car registration documents for the BMW, he was prompted to ask Edward about any car that Margaret may have had.

"Mr Culpebble, do you mind? You mentioned upstairs that your wife took her things away with her in a taxi. Did she not have her own car?"

"Margaret's car was purchased through the company I recently sold. Whether she had left me or not, it would have had to go. It was listed as an asset. Margaret wasn't in a position to buy it from the company and my financial position didn't allow me to offer her it at a knock-down price. I can give you my solicitor's details. He handled the sale of the lease to Mr Scott and the onward sale of the equipment to the refrigeration plant you mentioned across the county border. The car went in a private sale and the resulting fund reimbursed to my company, or more particularly, the bank."

"Would you write me a note of the address and contact number for your solicitor, Mr Culpebble? I'll check with him what you've just told me. He will hold the deeds to the house, will he?"

"No, those are with the mortgage company in Stenport. I'll add that information to the one for the solicitor."

"Thanks. Was your wife's life insured?"

"She might have done something for herself on a monthly subscription basis but she wasn't a joint owner of this property. Mine is the sole name on the deeds and mine is the life insured on the mortgage. She didn't contribute on that side of things."

"What would have happened to her if you'd died?"

"My estate would have passed to her by marriage. We didn't have any children. She is... was my sole beneficiary. That will be something I'll have to address with my solicitor. What about organising my wife's funeral, Inspector?"

"Her body won't be released for some time yet, Mr Culpebble. Reports on tests are still coming in. It all takes a long time, I'm afraid. Did Margaret leave any of her personal records behind?"

"We can double-check, if you like, but I'm certain she made up a file of everything and took it with her. I'd say go and check but I don't know where to direct you to."

"Your wife applied for leave of absence, you said, to

sort her head out, but records at DEFRA record your mother-in-law's death as the reason for needing compassionate leave."

"I can't explain that. She died five years ago. I'm surprised they don't know that already. Margaret was an only child. Her father died three years before that."

"Did she inherit?"

"Her parents sold a property to downsize. Her father had to go into residential care which took a fair chunk of the fund generated by the sale of the larger property. I took over the financial responsibility for the smaller house via my company, and when her mother died, the property was sold and my company reimbursed."

"That was quite involved, I daresay?"

"Yes indeed. Being the only child meant that Margaret took the brunt when both parents aged, which she was happy to do, of course. She was upset when her father went downhill so quickly. Her mother relied on her a great deal after that and for the last two years of her life."

At that point Andrew Raby came into the room to declare he'd finished scouring the attic.

"Did you find anything in that case Margaret left, Andy?"

"No, Sir. It was just women's clothes and underwear."

"If there's nothing useful for your investigation, is there any objection to me offloading the stuff at a charity shop, Inspector?"

"You're not in a rush, Mr Culpebble?"

"No indeed, not now, Inspector, but I've no use for her clothes myself. I just thought someone else might benefit."

"Give us until the end of the month, Mr Culpebble, and ask us again. While the investigation is at this early stage, you understand?"

"As you wish, Inspector."

"Right, Andy. Let's have a look at the garage and then we can leave Mr Culpebble in peace, for the time being. Is it locked, sir?"

"Yes, I'll open up for you."

Edward led the way through the ground floor to the inner garage door which he unlocked for the two policemen. Morrison and Raby worked systematically from the front to the back of the garage. Raby pointed out the garden brazier.

"This must be what he used out back for burning leaves. Mr Nelson said he did it twice over February and March was it?"

"Hm, hm."

"Are you going to ask him why he didn't call us, before we go?"

"Yes, Andy, and we'll find out what these are for."

"What's that, Sir?"

"The two cylinders. Ask him to come in, will you…?"

"Mr Culpebble. Can you tell us what these are for?"

"They're en route to the refrigeration plant at Whaitehouse."

"What's in them?"

"Ethyl chloride. It's used in refrigeration systems. I'll be taking them across after the weekend."

"I see. This brazier at the front of the garage. What do you use that for?"

"I do a hard cut-back of the shrubbery over autumn and in the new year. It all gets burned in spring."

"So you've used it this year then?"

"Yes, a couple of times."

"That's what Mr Nelson told us when we first called to see you and you were still away. Can you tell us, while I mention Mr Nelson, why you didn't make the contact when he gave you the number we'd left him?"

"I think there's a misunderstanding arising here, Inspector. Mr Nelson told me you had been asking questions. I understood you would be contacting me! If you hadn't come to see me when you did, I would have been asking Mr Nelson if he knew how to get in touch."

"I see. I thought he'd given you the number."

"No, Inspector. I think I would have rung if he had, don't you?"

"Yes, Mr Culpebble. That's what we were hoping."

Andrew looked at Morrison as Edward retreated back to his study. Andrew raised his eyebrows. Morrison nodded.

"We'll check with Mr Nelson just what the story is. Edward Culpebble sounds plausible in all respects, but we need to be sure. I'll go back to his study and ask him some more questions and you nip across to the Nelsons and see what Mr Nelson has to say. Don't relay anything about what Mr C has said. We don't want to plant suspicion where none may be needed at the moment."

"I'll just ask him to show us the number, Sir, and make out Culpebble rang and got a wrong number. Something along those lines, eh?"

"That sounds ok. See you shortly then, Andy."

Ten minutes later Raby returned and joined Morrison and Edward in the study. Morrison was concluding the visit, thanking Edward for his cooperation and arranging to keep him posted with any developments.

"I was just thinking, Sir, before we go, whether we

shouldn't take that case of clothes from the attic. If we have to stage a reconstruction or an appeal, it would be useful to have clothes that people might identify as belonging to Mrs Culpebble."

Edward interrupted before Morrison could comment on the suggestion.

"By all means, Mr Raby, but I don't know whether the contents of the case are Margaret's or her mother's."

"Yes, that may be so. Nevertheless, it's worth a punt. Were your wife and her mother of similar height and build, Mr Culpebble?"

"Margaret was a bit taller, like her father. Her mother was a tiny woman."

"Big in the bust like Margaret?"

"No, I think that came from the paternal grandmother."

"Run back upstairs, Andy. We'll take the case with us. Mr Culpebble, we'll send you a copy of the contents of the case and return it all to you when we're done with it. We'll be in touch."

Morrison held open the front door while Raby steered the case through the opening. Morrison shook Edward's hand and waved behind him as he walked to the car.

"So, what did Mr Nelson have to say?"

"He says he gave Mr C a paper with the number written on it, but, not having it any longer, he couldn't say whether he miscopied any digits in the number. He thought he'd copied it accurately but couldn't be certain."

"Did you check his original?"

"Yes, and it was fine."

"We're none the wiser, then. Both stories ring true. Mr N could have handed over the number, and Mr C could have been expecting us to contact him. Mrs Nelson shouldn't have been so generous, giving Culpebble the chance to ring before she did. This confusion of stories wouldn't have arisen, and we could have gauged his reactions on the spot. If he wanted time to prepare for us calling, he's had it."

"My feelings, Sir, are that either he's done her in, or the bloke she's been having an affair with has done the deed, or it's a completely random and vicious attack."

"All three scenarios are possible, Andy. Mr Culpebble could have a motive, the unknown lover could have a motive, if Margaret was threatening to expose their affair, and the body being found in Birkacre Woods suggests local knowledge, if our attacker is neither of the other two. She could have been making new contacts on social websites and met up with someone who only wanted to harm her."

"What does the corset suggest to you, Sir?"

"She's been dressed in the corset that she bought herself and her head has been shaved. That could be showing her as a woman of loose morals. They used to shave women's heads if they were found collaborating with an enemy, back in the day."

"That would tend more towards the betrayed husband and a random attacker than a lover… unless she betrayed him, too."

"We could speculate until the cows come home and still not know the answer. We'll see back at the office what Beryl has come up with. If she's got some names from the hotel in Cumbria, we can start to put pressure on to find out who the mystery bloke is."

Morrison had no sooner entered his team's working area than Beryl called him over.

"Sir! Take a look at what came back from Deer Horn

Inn while you were with Mr Culpebble."

Morrison read the email attachment and shared his look of surprise with Beryl's smile of acknowledgement.

"I'll ask him to come in, and we'll see if and how far he's involved."

"It's certainly an interesting new detail. You'll see, as well, that there were two calls from Mr Culpebble, evening and early morning. I've left the sheets in your office."

"Thanks, Beryl. Call together whoever's in, and we'll do a quick look where we are with this. Is Geoff in?"

"He's been arranging visits to the blokes on your list from the clinic. One of them was at home, and he had to telephone the other, older one to set up a meeting here at the station. I don't know if he's finished. I'll let him know you're back."

Chapter 17

Philip was glad to get home out of the rain that had hampered his work since late morning. The site visit with Councillor Stevens, the sixth now, was dragged out by having to keep sheltering from the heavy showers. He picked up the post and dumped his case and laptop in the study. He had accustomed himself to his own company whenever Gayle was away in Switzerland, but the absence of any contact with her had begun to leave him depressed.

While his defrosted ready meal cooked in the oven, he sifted through the day's post. He recognised the monthly bank statement and saw an envelope addressed to Gayle. He dropped the bank statement in preference for what turned out to be her credit card history for March. He sat down solidly on the kitchen chair as he read through the spending since he'd dropped her off at Whitelake airport on that fateful March afternoon. There was a hefty cancellation fee for the flight booking that Morrison had stopped on his behalf, but police or not, the fee was levied for lack of sufficient notice. There were further charges for a weekend break in the Lakes. He raised the contact number from the hotel's website, rang the number, gave dates and his wife's name as the person reserving the weekend deal and asked the receptionist to check who had been at the hotel that weekend. He was unnerved when the receptionist told him that a Mr Philip Innocent had been the guest that weekend. His claims that it couldn't have been him hadn't got him very far. The lady on reception advised him apologetically to check with his wife. When asked for a description, the lady couldn't help him, as she herself had been away that weekend, but promised to ring him with anything her stand-in colleague could remember. The reservation had been for single occupancy. What was Gayle playing at?

He was about to ring Morrison when his own mobile rang. It was Morrison himself.

"Inspector Morrison, I was just about to call you."

Philip explained in a rush of information what he had discovered in the post and what his call to the hotel had told him. Morrison tried to calm Philip so that he could take in what he was saying and make sense of it.

"This is a new development, Mr Innocent. It would be better if you could come in to the station. Bring the statement with you and I'll put one of my team on to checking with the card company how the reservation was made. It would be helpful to me to speak to you, as well, about another matter."

"Oh, what's that? Have you found anything more from my wife's computer?"

"We are following up on case files that we retrieved from her laptop, but I'll tell you about that when you come in. Can you make arrangements with your employers to meet me, let's say… ten tomorrow morning?"

"I'll be there, Inspector."

For the fifth time in two short months Philip stood at the counter in the small reception area at the station. His eyes drifted across to the information board where he had last seen the poster for the woman he had suggested might be Margaret Culpebble. He was struck by how their lives had touched in such different ways over a year. He was jolted out of his reflections as Morrison came through the back wall and lifted the counter for him to come through to the interview rooms off the corridor behind.

Once settled, facing Morrison across the desk, and business-like greetings having been exchanged, he handed across the details from the credit card statement he had been checking the previous evening.

"I'm completely confused by what's been going on. I called the hotel and they said that someone had stayed there under my own name. Though I've visited the Lakes and know many of the places to stay, I've never been at the Tarnside."

"You know the Deer Horn Inn then?"

"Yes, I've stayed there when overnighting on DEFRA business. Why do you ask?"

"I'll come back to that. If pushed, how would you be able to prove you were in Switzerland?"

"Why would I have to? What is this about?"

"Accommodate me, Mr Innocent."

"I bought a flight, booked a hotel, visited the Staatsklink, went to the police and the rest, trying to find anyone or anything that might tell me where Gayle was."

"Ok. Give me a moment while I get someone to deal with this hotel."

Morrison left the interview room. Philip felt a shift in the atmosphere that he couldn't quite explain and felt a slight unease; the reference to the Deer Horn Inn, the need to prove he'd been in Switzerland. He braced himself to be mentally alert, knowing he was at the disadvantage of not knowing where Morrison was coming from. His thoughts were about where Gayle might be and how she was. The obvious link didn't register until Morrison was back behind the desk.

"You know and did some work with Margaret Culpebble."

"I did. Yes. What's that got to do with Gayle?"

"How long have you known Margaret Culpebble?"

"I think she's been at DEFRA offices in Stenport for three years. I don't know where she was before that. She was part of a team that worked on the foot-and-mouth outbreak and its repercussions. She attended several meetings with me across last year."

"You stayed at the Deer Horn Inn on the same night that Margaret was there. Tell me about that, Mr Innocent."

"What's there to tell beyond that? I was working for DEFRA on the information-gathering exercise after that isolated outbreak across Northern England. Margaret was there to assist. We had meetings during the day and following day with representatives of all aspects of concern via Cumbria County Council offices, and Deer Horn Inn was the hotel of convenience."

"Anyone else from DEFRA or the people you had meetings with staying there?"

"Just the two of us on that occasion. The main work to isolate and limit the outbreak had been done earlier. I was moving on to Sheffield for further meetings. Margaret Culpebble was returning to base at Stenport."

"Separate rooms, Mr Innocent?"

"Look! What is this? Of course separate rooms."

"Were you and Margaret Culpebble connected in any way other than as colleagues?"

"Of course not, Inspector. I resent the implication. I love my wife and I'm more worried about what's happened to her than, pardon me, Margaret Culpebble, however sorry I am that she's dead."

"So you and Margaret didn't sleep together or visit each other in your rooms?"

"My god! Where are you going with this? I came in about Gayle."

"Please answer the question, Mr Innocent."

"No!"

"Did you eat together? Have a drink in the bar? Anything like that?"

"Yes. It was a long day; lots of feedback from meetings to collate. We took a quick meal break and then carried on afterwards."

"Did Margaret take any calls while you were working together?"

"Not while we were together, no. I can't say if she spoke to anyone when she was back in her room. What are you getting at?"

"Did Margaret speak to anyone else at the hotel?"

"I can't see that there was much time to do that but I wasn't there to watch her every move after we'd called it a day."

"Did you work together in the early morning?"

"How early is early, Inspector? We met up after breakfast. That would have been after nine. I asked her to drive us to the first of that day's meetings. That would have been at ten in Carlisle."

"Could you explain for me how her husband, who rang her about six thirty, heard another person, a male, in the room with her?"

Philip felt he was reaching the edge of a dark place with the trend of the questioning but decided to continue, for self-preservation's sake, with his denials of involvement.

"I'm certain I would still have been soundly asleep at that time. Could Margaret have had the radio on, maybe? Did Edward hear someone on the radio?"

"You know her husband, then?"

"I know his name, yes. I've never met him, though."

"Do you know a Muriel Turnbill, Mr Innocent?"

"I've heard the name. Who is she?"

"Margaret told her husband she was sharing a room with her, but the voice he heard was male… and it wasn't the radio he heard."

"Whatever Margaret got up to that night after we went to our respective rooms I can't help you with, Inspector. Whatever story she has told her husband, it's nothing to do with me."

"We are investigating a murder, Mr Innocent. You found the body and had links with the murdered woman. You fall into a range of people we would treat as suspects."

"Well, what about my wife? She's the one I came in to see you about. She's missing and someone is spending her money against our joint account, impersonating me in the Lakes. How can you help me with that?"

"We can arrange with the company to put a block on further transactions, in case her card's been stolen and being used fraudulently. You can have a word with your bank. Is her salary still being paid?"

"I haven't checked that out, as yet. She would only be paid a token retainer fee by the local clinic while she's in Switzerland. I frankly don't know how the Swiss arrangement would work out, if she's not there seeing clients. I'll have to get on to them and see how things stand. It's been a month now and not a word from Gayle."

"Is she punishing you for something, going off like this? It's not unknown."

"If there was something, I don't know about it, and with her being a trained therapist, I would expect her to be able to talk about any problem she might be having."

"That might be true of her relationship with clients, but she might find it more difficult to deal in the same way with you as her husband. Can you think of anything that would change her behaviour so radically? Any health issue that's arisen? Death of someone she's close to?"

"I can't think of anything. I'll have a word with Laura, her sister, but both her parents are now dead. Her mother died when she was sixteen and her father about two years ago. Do I have to consider, Inspector, that my wife has left the country, started a new life somewhere else, be dead even?"

"I can't give you a definite answer either way, Mr Innocent. Whether blocking her card from our end and you doing the same with your joint account will flush out a response from your wife, well, only time will tell. In the meantime, if you have a photo of yourself we can show that to the hotelier and see if it prompts a memory."

Philip handed over his ID badge for Morrison to scan.

"Is there anything I can be doing to find my wife, Inspector?"

"There was nothing that came out from that list of friends of hers that we checked. The reaction was of complete surprise that she was missing. You could check your list again, perhaps with help from your sister-in-law, to come up with additional names. I have to warn you, Mr Innocent, if your wife doesn't want to be found, there's not much we'll be able to do."

"What did you make of him?"

Morrison sought out Beryl in the viewing room after he'd seen Philip Innocent out through the station's reception area.

"He came across to me as two individuals: one desperate to find his missing wife and the other who probably paired up with Margaret Culpebble when they did that overnight together outside Carlisle. My gut instinct is he's lying about that. When I spoke to her colleagues at Stenport there was a nudge and a wink in the direction of our Mr Innocent. I had a word with Muriel Turnbill, checking out Mr Culpebble's story of meeting her in the supermarket that evening, and she said that Philip had a bit of a reputation. Not a groper but not averse, if it was offered to him on a plate. I don't think he's our killer. Young man at a loose end months at a time, I wonder how many notches he has on hotel bedposts. I'm surprised he lied though. It will come back to slap him in the face like these things always do. Do you think he killed her, sir?"

"It's as much a possibility as anybody else at this stage. Anything back from other forces on our poster of her?"

"Nil returns, as yet. We'll have to keep digging."

"What a wonderful range of encouragement you draw on, Beryl."

"It's like growing veg, Sir. Dig in the right patch and you reap nature's rewards."

"Let's not get bogged down in you knowing your onions, Beryl. Did you get a statement from Muriel Turnbill?"

"I just made notes."

"Get back to her. I'd like something on paper if we have to re-interview Mr Innocent about his liaisons dangéreuses."

Chapter 18

DC Waller dialled the number for the Cavendish Clinic.

"I'd like to speak to Miss Lester, if she's working today."

"Speaking."

"Hi. It's Geoff here."

"Geoff who?"

"Detective Constable Waller at your service."

"Sorry. I didn't recognise your voice."

"I wanted to call at the clinic to ask you some questions about one of Dr Innocent's clients."

"Shouldn't you speak to Mrs Cavendish?"

"It's not likely Mrs Cavendish would be able to help, if he wasn't her client, and Dr Innocent isn't available, so I was wondering if I could call at lunchtime. Do you have to man the reception over lunchtime?"

"No, we close between one and two."

"I'll see you at one then. I should be finished here by then. Mention to Mrs Cavendish that I'll be calling and why."

"Which client do you have in mind? Tell me and I'll look up their file."

"I have all the details I need from the file. It's a case of whether you can recall what he looked like. You don't keep photo ID with your files."

"Who's the client?"

"Rowan McCord. Had a couple of appointments with Dr Innocent just before the fourteenth of March."

"I'll check his dates and see if I can think who it was and what he looked like. I have an idea."

"That would be very helpful. I'll see you about one. Bye."

It was ten past one when he walked into reception.

"Sorry I'm late. Do you want to grab a bite while we talk about Mr McCord? I'm starving. I saw a pub down the road which looked reasonably quiet."

"Sure. Is it on your expenses then DC Waller?"

"It can be. I'll leave my car here, if that's ok? It's only a short walk…"

"What do you fancy? Let me get you a drink."

"Thanks. I'll have the quiche and salad with a white wine."

"I'll give the steak and mushroom pie a go. Do you want chips with your quiche?"

"Best not, eh! I'll watch while you eat yours."

After chatting while they ate lunch, Geoff asked Bowie, Barbara Lester, if she could remember anything about Rowan McCord.

"Yes. I had a look at his appointment listings and I can remember him as an older man than most who come to the clinic. I'd say he was in his fifties. He was on the tall side. How tall are you?"

"Six foot. I'll stand up then you can gauge whether he was taller, shorter or whatever."

"Looking at you, I'd say he was slightly shorter. What would that be? Five ten, eleven, maybe?"

"How would you describe his build?"

"Quite slim. He had fair hair, pale ginger; certainly not dark."

"You've a good memory, Bowie."

"I remembered him from his smile when he came in for his appointments. Really white teeth, like he looked after them or had had work done."

"I see."

Geoff made notes.

"Oh, and he had a long nose… and he had almond eyes."

"Almond eyes? What colour is that?"

"No. Their shape was like an almond. I think he had blue eyes. What's all this for? Is this to do with Dr Innocent being away?"

"I can't say, Bowie. I've tried contacting all Dr Innocent's clients, and he's the only one I haven't been able to speak to. Neither his address nor his phone contact details are of any use. He didn't have a number listed on his file, and his address turned out to be a student let."

"I see. Well, I hope my description helps you to find him. Look at the time! I'll have to be back on duty."

"Thanks for your help… Do you fancy a drink with me when all this business is over?"

Geoff took a note of her mobile number, saying he would contact her sometime, and walked back along the road with her to the clinic.

He reported back in with DI Morrison when he got back to Belton Station. No joy with the Lakes hotel. Sign-in time clocked at seventeen thirty-eight but the stand-in receptionist had no memory of Mr Innocent even from being shown his photo.

"Does the hotel have CCTV?"

"I don't know if they have any but I'll ring them and double-check."

"If they have it in reception, Geoff, ask them for a copy of their CCTV for the Friday half five registration period. If it's big enough they should have cameras outside, if not inside. If our Mr Innocent is not as innocent as he seems, we'll soon find out."

Geoff gave Dermond Morrison the details of the description of Rowan McCord which Bowie Lester had given him. After ribbing him about organising his courting on police time, Morrison told him to add the details to the Gayle Innocent file.

"Mr Culpebble has ultra-white teeth, too. You never know, they might both use the same dental practice."

"Does he? I've never seen him."

Chapter 19

The doorbell rang. Philip closed the file he was working on and went to open the door to greet Laura, his sister-in-law. He batted away two large black flies exploring a route out into the open air on the glass panel at the side of the door.

"Come in. Nice to see you. Thanks for coming over. It's a good job you didn't bring Lily. The flies have multiplied in the warmer weather. You know how she throws one when anything buzzes round her."

"Phew! Take my bag will you, Phil?"

She gave Philip a hug and moved towards the lounge to sit down, even though she'd been sitting on the train and in the taxi to get over from Derbyshire.

"Do you want a cuppa?"

"I'd love a coffee. Milk, no sugar, please."

Philip organised a tray for them both and returned to the lounge.

"How long are you staying?"

"I get the train back tomorrow. Lily's got a Parents' Evening on the Monday I don't want to miss."

"Have you eaten?"

"I had something before I set off. This will do. I need to lose some weight now we're into the warmer weather. These biscuits are scrummy though."

"How's David? Does he mind being in charge while you are here?"

"He's fine. It will do him good to manage himself and Lily for the day. I think he was talking about taking her fishing."

Laura swiped away another of the black flies that had landed on her plate of biscuits.

"That's ginormous!"

"I think they've hatched early in the roof space with our warm spell. They die off quickly. There's a couple of them on the kitchen window ledge."

"Tell me about how you got on with Morrison."

"Like I was telling you, I took in the credit card statement that showed me taking a weekend break in the Lakes when I was nowhere near the place. I got a grilling about the woman whose body I found in Birkacre Woods. It was like I was juggling between two interviews. The woman worked in the DEFRA team around the North. They were trying to pin down anyone who knew her. I know the woman's dead, in probably a horrible way, but Gayle is my concern. Morrison said he would arrange to get her card stopped. I've been into the bank to explain but they won't just take my word for it. There's stuff I'll have to do via the police and my solicitor. If her card's been stolen and being used fraudulently, whoever has it could clear the account. It's bad enough Gayle being missing without having the threat of not being able to run this house and pay the mortgage."

"Do the police know of any more spends against the card?"

"I'm waiting to hear from them. I'd given them details of our friends around here that they've interviewed, all of whom are completely surprised that she's missing."

"As are we."

"He wanted to know if she had any health problem that was worrying her, or if someone had died, someone she was close to. I told him both her parents were dead. Had she mentioned anything to you? You know, women's things that she might feel more comfortable speaking to you about before she said anything to me?"

"Not a thing, Phil, and there's no-one our side of the M6 who's died that I know of whom Gayle might have been upset about – enough to hide away, at any rate. Were you two solid, Phil?"

"Of course we were. This thing's a complete mystery to me. We were going to meet up in Basle, have a long weekend together, do the quality time thing."

"And there's nothing been going on with anybody else?"

"No. You're as bad as the police."

"It's something that needs to be asked. David was saying the same thing. Why else would Gayle just suddenly disappear? Had you had an argument?"

"The police asked me the same kind of questions, but the answer to you and David, as it was to the police, is no. Gayle wouldn't deal with a situation by running away from it. She was measured and reflective and would question things."

"But remember, you told me that she had been a bit off before you gave her a lift to Whitelake."

"Yes, but it was nothing significant. I put it down to PMT."

"Or there could have been something that she was

beginning to worry about."

"That's something I've gone over again and again till it does my head in. Did I miss anything? Has she had an accident and is lying somewhere undiscovered?"

"At Whitelake airport?"

"She has to have gone somewhere else because her flight was booked for three days later on the seventeenth."

"Where though? And why tell you she was travelling on the fourteenth? Did the police get anywhere with CCTV at the airport?"

"The camera was being replaced at the entrance closest to the drop-off layby. There's nothing from the inside of the terminal that suggests she even went inside."

"Did she take a taxi? Have the police checked with the firms who have a contract with the airport?"

"Yes, and then no."

"What do you mean?"

"Yes they've checked and no – nobody of Gayle's name or description took a fare that afternoon."

"Somebody else must have picked her up. Her car's still here, I take it?"

"It is, but who might that somebody else be?"

"A client? Someone she was having an affair with?"

"Oh God, Laura, don't say that. The police lifted names of her recent clients – since she came back last November – and have been interviewing those they can find."

"Well, we'll have a good think between us tomorrow. I need to use your loo."

Laura finished her coffee and said she would unpack her overnight bag and call it a day. Philip carried her bag upstairs and showed her the spare room she would sleep in and the bathroom at her disposal.

"What's that whiff?"

"It's probably with the house being sealed up while I'm at work and the warm spell we've been having."

"It smells different from that. Have you put any bleach down the plugholes lately?"

"I'll do that tomorrow. Sleep well. 'Night."

Laura closed the door on him. Philip stood on the landing and sniffed to try and identify what Laura had noticed.

Chapter 20

"How did you get on with the hotel CCTV?"

"They've nothing set up at Tarnside. It's not much bigger than a B&B. The regular receptionist was off on the date given. She's tried to get a description from the young woman standing in for her, but it's all a bit vague, Sir: tall, wearing outdoor gear hikers go in for; couldn't give his hair colour because he was wearing a woollen hat that covered his head; blue eyes and a nice smile."

Geoff Waller finished reading from his notebook.

"Did he use a card to buy anything?"

"No, Sir. What I did get from them was the landline number the weekend was booked from."

Geoff spelt out the digits of the number.

"Hang on a minute. That sounds familiar. Have you checked it out yourself yet?"

Morrison's mobile rang. He recognised Edward Culpebble's number.

"Mr Culpebble. How can I help you?"

"I'm ringing because I'm hoping I might be able to help you."

"I'm listening, Mr C."

"When you came to my house to conduct the search I told you that I'd sent the shoes that Margaret left behind to the charity shop but that I still had to sort out her books."

"Yes, Mr Culpebble."

"Well, Inspector, I was doing just that yesterday evening and found something tucked inside one of the books I was checking. I don't know whether it will be of any use but I thought I'd better mention it."

"Go on, Mr Culpebble."

"As I was upending a book to shake out anything that might be in it, before the charity shop sold it on, some photos and a folded sheet fell on the floor."

"How might they help us, sir?"

"The photos won't. They are of Margaret's father and mother, but when I opened up the sheet of paper it showed a DEFRA heading and there was rather a strange message."

"Have you got it there?"

"Yes. Shall I read it?"

Morrison listened to Edward relaying the content of the message to Margaret from someone signing off as Philip.

"Thank you, Mr Culpebble. Please hold on to it, and I'll send one of my Detective Constables over to collect it. It could be useful in finding who it was Margaret was seeing from the DEFRA team."

"That's what I was wondering, too, Inspector Morrison."

Just as Morrison was finishing the call, Geoff came back into his office.

"I've got the name for the landline number you told me to check, sir."

"Ok then, Geoff. Surprise me. Who is it?"

"It comes up as Mr P Innocent."

"Well done, Geoff! Take the address details from Margaret Culpebble's file and get down there straight away. Her husband's just been in touch with me about a letter he's found. Put it in an evidence bag and bring it back here. We'll have a look at it and get it over to forensics. Is Andy here?"

"No, but Beryl is."

"Ask her to come in on your way out, there's a good lad."

Morrison dispatched Beryl to collect a warrant to search Philip Innocent's home.

Morrison rang Philip Innocent and arranged an evening time to come and update him about their investigations. He had cut short Philip's attempts to get details over the phone. He felt a measure of sympathy for the man, eager to discover what had happened to his wife but this was tempered by his irritation at Philip's lying about Margaret Culpebble. His instinct, honed over years of investigating crime, told him Mr Innocent was lying.

Morrison's team, including Andy, Beryl and Constable Winch, waited at Philip's front door just before six pm. Philip looked in surprise at the number of people assembled there when he opened it wide. All of the group, with the exception of Constable Winch, went into the lounge. Constable Winch took up a position outside the lounge door. When they were all seated Philip looked expectantly at Morrison.

"You've come to tell me that you've found my wife. Am I right?"

"No, Mr Innocent, unfortunately not. My name is Detective Constable Gillibrand and I've come to ask you why you've been lying to us about Margaret Culpebble and your relationship with her."

"I thought you had some news for me about my wife. I had no relationship with Margaret Culpebble beyond working with her."

"But you did sleep with her?"

"Where are you going with this?"

"Did you or did you not sleep with Margaret Culpebble at the Deer Horn Inn?"

"I have nothing to say on that matter. It's irrelevant to her being dead. I found her body, though I didn't know it at the time. I gave you information when I saw the poster and that helped towards identifying the body as Margaret Culpebble, but all of that is much less important to me than where and why my wife is missing. I have nothing to do with Margaret's death."

"Maybe your wife found out that you had been carrying on with Margaret."

Philip stood up in exasperation.

"I've invited you into my house to hear an update on my wife's disappearance, not to listen to supposition and innuendo about another woman."

"You have a reputation, Mr Innocent, among the female staff at DEFRA in Stenport."

Philip looked bewildered.

"What are you insinuating, DC Gillibrand?"

"The description from people we spoke to said, while you are not a groper, you wouldn't say no to something being offered to you on a plate."

"That's just tittle-tattle. I'm surprised the police have

time for gossip like that."

Morrison interrupted the exchange.

"You're right of course, Mr Innocent. We are dealing with a known murder and your wife's disappearance. It is just coming to light that you are an important link."

"What? How?"

"One of my Detective Constables is at this moment collecting written evidence of that link with Margaret Culpebble, and I and my colleagues are now going to present you with a warrant to search this property to see if further evidence exists."

"I need to get in touch with a solicitor, if you are going to do that."

"There'll be time for that, if we find anything, Mr Innocent. You will stay here with Constable Winch while my colleagues and I search your property. I suggest you sit down. Constable Winch!"

He came into the room at Morrison's call. Beryl ducked away from a large black fly that zoomed through from the hall.

"Mind yourself, Beryl. There's a few more buzzing around out there."

Constable Winch positioned himself against the door in the lounge while the others dispersed through the house...

Philip's body tightened when he heard a man's voice shout from upstairs. He went to stand up but the constable gestured to him to remain sitting.

"Sir, Beryl, up here!"

The two colleagues left where they were searching and moved upstairs quickly to the spot on the landing where the ladder to the attic rested on the carpet. Morrison climbed first to peer into the darkened space of the attic, to where an LED torchlight showed where Raby was.

"What have you found, Andy?"

Even as he posed the question, his nose was beginning to suggest an answer.

"There's something here wrapped up in a sheet and thick polythene. We need some better light to make out what it is. There's an unmistakeable pong coming from it, whatever it is."

"I think, Andy, you mean whoever it is. I'll get Beryl to alert the technical people. I wonder if we haven't found Gayle Innocent."

He gave instructions to Andy to wait in the house for the SOCOs and Forensics to arrive and do their job, and for Beryl to call the teams in and then return with him to Belton station. They would take Mr Innocent there for further questioning. With these arrangements agreed, the three officers walked into the lounge.

"Mr Innocent, have you your house keys available?"

"Yes. Why?"

"DS Raby here will take them from you and be responsible for checking that your house is secure after our teams have finished their further search of your attic."

"My attic? Why my attic?"

"We have reason to suppose that there is something decomposing there. That will explain the flies we've seen around your house and the smell around the first floor."

"Laura, Gayle's sister, said something similar last weekend when she was over. Do you mean like rats or birds?"

Morrison looked at Philip, wondering if he was making fun of them.

"No, Mr Innocent. I believe we may be dealing with human remains."

Philip stepped backwards in horrified surprise and,

overbalancing against the front of the armchair, fell into it.

"Go with Constable Winch, Mr Innocent, and get a jacket. You will be coming back to the station with us for further questioning."

"I want someone to represent me in that case."

"At this stage you will be helping us with our enquiries. If it comes to charging you with anything, your rights will be made clear to you."

Leaving Andy waiting for Forensics and SOCOs to arrive, Morrison drove the rest back to Belton station.

He opened the interview room that Philip was now quite familiar with and asked Barbara to organise a drink for him. He looked to check if Geoff had returned.

DC Waller was sifting through files at his desk.

"I'm glad I caught you, Geoff. Did you get the letter from Edward Culpebble?"

"I did. I put it in an evidence bag and left it in your office."

"What does it say?"

"A chap signing himself as Philip says to Margaret that the fun is over. There's the DEFRA office heading on the sheet."

"Handwritten?"

"No, typed."

"You mean printed off a computer?"

"No... uh... I didn't really look."

The two men collected the sheet in its evidence sleeve and scrutinised it without touching it.

"Turn it over and see if the letters have impressed on the paper."

Geoff took a set of tweezers from a drawer and drew

the sheet out of the sleeve.

"Yep, Sir. See for yourself."

"Well, well, well. Who uses a typewriter these days? Put it back in its sleeve and I'll hear what Mr Innocent has to say. Are you working late tonight?"

Geoff shook his head.

"I'll leave this in the Culpebble folder on my desk. First thing tomorrow whip it over to Forensics and get them to check it for prints. Enjoy what's left of the evening, you lucky man, you."

"Wilco, Sir. See you tomorrow."

Morrison took the letter in its evidence sleeve to make a copy of it and left Philip Innocent to take stock of his position.

A call came through from Andy at about 9.30 p.m.

"Hi, Sir. Dr Dayton and his team got here quite quickly and they've taken the body away for examination. They're going over the attic and house with a fine-tooth comb, too."

"Did you get a chance to look at the body?"

"Dr Dayton said the body was closely wrapped in polythene and covered again with a black fabric sheet. He opened the end where the head was. It's our missing lady. He's estimating at the moment that she's been here between six and ten weeks. He wanted to keep the body and wrapping as intact as possible till he gets her across to Stenport for the post-mortem."

"Good work, Andy. I'll prime uniform to send a car for you when the technical team have finished for the night. Bye."

He collected Beryl from her workstation and briefed her about Andy's call before they entered the interview room.

"Mr Innocent. I wonder, while you've been sitting here waiting, whether you've had any thoughts about the story you've told us?"

"In what respect?"

"I mean, Mr Innocent, what kind of a relationship existed between you and Margaret Culpebble."

"I've told you, Inspector. There wasn't one."

"Did your wife find out that you two had been having an affair?"

"NO! What do I have to say to convince you?"

"The truth, Mr Innocent. This is not a game. We are looking at a link between two murders. And you're the link."

"What do you mean by two murders?"

"As you've been sitting waiting, Dr Dayton, the pathologist, has been to your house and uncovered the remains of your wife, Gayle."

The shock registered physically in Philip's body. The colour drained from his face and he looked like he was going to slump in a faint.

"Get some water, Beryl."

Morrison and Winch bent Philip's head over his knees. Beryl came back in with the water. After he had recovered, he burst into tears.

"Please… no… not Gayle. No… please, not Gayle."

"I'm sorry, Mr Innocent, but Dr Dayton says she's been in your attic between six and ten weeks. Do you want to tell me about that?"

"I'm not saying any more until I have a solicitor to represent me. I'm frightened by where you are leading me."

"In that case, Mr Innocent, I am going to detain you for further questioning about the murder of your wife, Gayle, and the suspected murder of Margaret Culpebble. Read him his rights, Beryl, while I get one of the duty solicitors in for him. Set up for taped interviews as per."

Morrison and Beryl returned to the interview room after the duty solicitor, Adam Wilson, had had time to discuss the charge with Philip.

The tape was switched on and, after preliminaries timed and dated the interview and participants, Morrison recapped the suspicions based within the twin lines of questioning.

"Mr Innocent. The pathologist, Dr Dayton, has estimated that your wife, now dead, has been in your attic from anything between six and ten weeks. You've been unaware of that?"

"I've never been in the attic space since Christmas. My sister-in-law was over last weekend and she mentioned a smell on the landing. I put that down to the house being totally closed up while I've been at work, and particularly during this hot spell."

"The time scale for her being stored there fits around the time you say you gave your wife a lift to Whitelake airport. Do you agree?"

"You could say so. I dropped her off on the fourteenth of March for an afternoon flight to Basle where she was starting her three-month stint at the clinic."

"And yet, Mr Innocent, the actual flight was set for late afternoon on the seventeenth."

"I told YOU that when I found out she hadn't arrived and did some digging around for an explanation."

"Unfortunately, there's no evidence of that drop-off. Your wife is likely to have been dead by the seventeenth, and your 'digging around', as you call it, could be an inventive cover for your having killed her."

"I can't be blamed for how Whitelake manages its camera security, and why would I want to kill my wife? I love her."

"Let's look at why you might have killed her. You found Margaret Culpebble's body in a little-visited part of Birkacre Woods. A bit of a coincidence, wouldn't you say?"

"It was a completely random chance that my visit to check over that part for the trustees led to my finding her body. I wish I'd never been there that afternoon. I don't think I would be sitting here now."

"You mean, you hope you would have got away with it."

"I'll spell it out to you and anybody anywhere who wants to listen. I DID NOT KILL HER. If I had killed her, why would I be reporting finding a body to you the next day?"

"You're an intelligent man, Mr Innocent. You may have planned all this to cover the two murders. You spent time away with Margaret Culpebble. What was the nature of your relationship?"

"I've made no secret about working with Margaret as a member of our team and, towards the end of the work generated by the foot-and-mouth outbreak, staying overnight with just her. I've nothing to hide about that. We were working. End of. That's all there was to it."

"We have evidence that you are, perhaps, hiding the true nature of that relationship."

"And that evidence is?"

"We have a letter you sent to Margaret that is highly suggestive of more between you and her than you are admitting here."

The duty solicitor, Adam Wilson, asked to see the evidence. Beryl handed over, from the file in front of her, a photocopy of the item yet to be examined by Forensics. She announced the same to the tape recorder. Philip asked to look at the item, too and looked aghast at the sheet, the heading and the message.

"This photocopy is of a letter found in a search of Margaret Culpebble's address. Let me read you the message."

"You don't need to. I've read the message and I swear I never wrote it. It's an invention."

"By whom? For what reason?"

"I can't imagine?"

"What kind of fun can she be talking about? The camaraderie and unity of purpose you find in a good team, sorting out the after-effects on farmers and associated groups of the foot-and-mouth outbreak?"

Philip remained silent.

"How did Margaret feel about being dumped because you had Gayle to consider?"

Philip sat with his forehead in his left hand, the fingers rubbing to and fro; his head turning against them in a counter rhythm.

"Why would Margaret keep something like that?"

"I've no idea."

"Was she threatening to let your wife know what you two had been up to? It supports the link between the two murders."

"I'm not going to make any comment that's going to give any credence to the links you are inventing. I worked with Margaret. I didn't kill her. I love my wife. I didn't kill her. What are you doing to find the person or people who've done all this? IT ISN'T ME."

"Where were you on the weekends of the twentieth and twenty-seventh of March?"

"Why?"

"Just answer the question."

"The twentieth, which you know about already, I was in Basle trying to find my wife."

"So you have said. And the twenty-seventh?"

"I was at home."

"Can you explain, Mr Innocent, why the second weekend, paid for on your wife's card, was booked from your home phone?"

"That's impossible."

"I'm afraid, Mr Innocent, the phone records show that the call registered to your landline, booking the weekend break, was made on the afternoon of the eighteenth. You had been in with me in the morning to report your wife's non-arrival in Switzerland. Do you remember?

"I do indeed but I'll need to check where I was later on that day. At what time was the call made?"

"I think we'll wait to hear from you about where you were and what you were doing."

"I'm only trying to be helpful, Inspector. I didn't make that call. I promise you."

"And if I didn't, who did?"

"You said it yourself, sir. What we have is a scenario of you in a relationship with Mrs Culpebble; you saying the relationship is over and Margaret probably making threats to disclose the relationship. That posed a risk with Gayle. Maybe she did find out and threatened to leave you, so you had to get rid of her, too."

"It all sounds far-fetched to me. If it weren't so serious, I'd laugh it off as farcical."

"You may be thinking you're leading the police by the nose, claiming your wife's missing and at the same time putting forward evidence for her being alive to cover your involvement in her death and that of Margaret, too."

"Tell me the evidence that links their deaths to me."

"Even as we are talking, Mr Innocent, we're on that job, and you will be detained while we do it. Beryl, book him in with the duty Sergeant and arrange for prints and DNA samples to be taken."

His mobile rang, and he left the interview room to go to his office to take the call.

"It's me, Sir."

"Hi, Andy. How are you getting on?"

"It's why I'm ringing you, sir. I was going through papers and files in a downstairs office and I've found a letter from Margaret Culpebble addressed to Philip Innocent."

"Have you now? Let me get something to write this down… Go ahead, Andy. Read me all the hearts and flowers stuff, if that's what it is."

Andy read out slowly the pleas of Margaret Culpebble to carry on meeting outside of working arrangements; how the sex with him had made her come alive again as a woman; how she didn't want to lose the thrill of their physical contact; how she didn't want it to end.

"Oh, be still my beating heart. Where did you find it?"

"It was in a file on the development of Birkacre Woods. It was full of emails, diagrams and technical reports. It just slipped out from among the sheets while I was leafing through."

"Well spotted, Andy. Bring it back here with you. Have you any interested parties from the media hanging around?"

"Not yet. They'll be here soon enough. How's Innocent taking all this? Have you spoken to him yet?"

"I've just sent him for prints and DNA. We'll keep at him. He's still lying through his teeth about what was going on with Margaret Culpebble. This will shake him up."

Chapter 21

Morrison spent the following morning organising his team to do checks on the dates of the two weekends, while he went off to Dayton's pathology premises in Stenport.

Beryl was to check Philip's movements, and Geoff was to check flight details for the Basle weekend. Andy, continuing the search of Philip's property with the SOCOs, was to check with neighbours and contact Laura Prendergast, Philip's sister-in-law, to arrange to call the next day. They would all liaise around the end of the shift at 6 p.m.

Their pool of findings raised more than one pair of eyebrows.

Morrison opened the review with Dr Dayton's findings thus far. The murder of Gayle Innocent followed a similar pattern to that of Margaret Culpebble: pressure asphyxiation after chemically-induced unconsciousness. Further checks were underway for any residual fibres, to see if they matched the findings in Margaret's case. The body, bare of clothing, had been wrapped in polythene and moved soon after death up to the attic at Philip Innocent's property. Time of death tied in with the last sighting of her in mid-March.

Geoff reported the early morning outward flight to Basle for the nineteenth and the late evening return on the twenty-second.

Beryl stirred interest in the group when she reported that, while Philip Innocent claimed to be in Basle the weekend starting the nineteenth, he failed to inform them that he had returned to Manchester on the twentieth. Bernard Pascoe, his boss at EnviroOptions, had had to call him back from leave to meet two councillors, Mr Stevens and Mr Gore, making a last-minute request for a report before an important debate on the waste incineration project that had been brought forward to the following Monday. She had confirmed with Mr Gore that this was the case, and the venue for their meeting was the Manchester Quays Hotel. Geoff was primed to go there the next day and get a copy of the Saturday tape, if the three men were shown there. Beryl was to accompany Andy down to Derbyshire to meet Laura Prendergast and arrange for her to identify Gayle's body.

With the solicitor, Adam Wilson, installed alongside Philip Innocent in the interview room, Morrison and Andy Raby took up the chairs facing them across the table. Morrison set the tape running to record this second interview…

"Is there anything, Mr Innocent, that you wish to change or add to the details you've already given us?"

"No. I can't account for any reason why I should be held here. My wife, you tell me, is dead. I didn't kill her. How did she die? Was it over quickly?"

"Interesting you should ask me that. The killing of your wife, Gayle, is, from what we know so far, following the same method used to kill Margaret Culpebble."

"Have you thought about anybody else who might have done the killings? Mr Culpebble, for example?"

"Mr Culpebble has already been questioned and his property searched. What link would there be between him and your wife?"

"I don't know. Was he one of her clients at the clinic?"

"I'm afraid not, and anything he has volunteered so far has checked out. If only we could say the same about you."

"I didn't write the letter you produced last time."

"Tell me about the weekend of the twenty/twenty-first, the first one after you dropped your wife at Whitelake to go off to Switzerland."

"I told you. I'd time off booked, so I went to Basle, as planned, to try and find her."

"But you didn't tell us quite the full story, did you?"

"As much as would apply to Gayle's disappearance."

"Detective Constable Gillibrand, whom you've met, spoke with your boss at EnviroOptions. He told her that you came back from Basle over that weekend. Did you not think to mention that?"

"There was no point. I was in the UK and out again in twenty-four hours. I arrived in Manchester, met Mr Gore and Mr Stevens. There was a last-minute request from them. I met them at the Manchester Quays Hotel, worked with them till quite late, stayed overnight and left early the next morning."

"And your wife's card wasn't used for that?"

"Of course not. Nor mine, for that matter. Bernard Pascoe authorised the flights from Enviro accounts and the councillors stood the bill for my hotel stay. I wasn't anywhere near my home till I got back late on Monday the twenty-second."

"The following weekend you say you were at home. Yet none of the people we've spoken to remember seeing anything of you, even your closest neighbour, Mrs Andrea Swarbrick."

"Her not remembering and me not being at home are not the same thing. Are they, Inspector? I was coming to a final recommendation report for Manchester City Council – I'd briefed Gore and Stevens the previous weekend for a debate on the Monday. A written full report was needed sharpish for circulation for another decisive meeting coming up. I kept my head down all that weekend to make sure it was finished."

"And yet nobody saw you. Now, Mr Innocent, my colleague, DS Raby, will show you and Mr Wilson something he found at your house as part of our search."

DS Raby passed across the photocopy of the letter he had unearthed. He announced the same to the tape. After studying it between them, Philip reached the sheet back across the table.

"You never found this in my house, DS Raby. And do you know why? I never received it. How do I know it's not been something you've planted?"

"It was found in among your file of papers on Birkacre Woods and photographed by one of the Scene of Crime Officers working alongside me."

"Somebody else put it there then."

Morrison picked up the lead questioning again

"We have to ask you again, Mr Innocent. Who and why? The letter gives clear evidence that you were sexually involved with Margaret Culpebble which you have repeatedly denied. More than one person has hinted that you were happy to play away, despite saying to us that you loved your wife. You yourself found the body in Birkacre Woods, and your own wife has been dead in your attic from around the date you said you last saw her AND you were the last person to see her alive. A lot of reasonable people other than myself would readily say your story is a tissue of lies."

Chapter 22

Beryl Gillibrand and Andrew Raby waited outside the front door of Laura Prendergast's home after ringing the doorbell. They became aware of a figure coming down the stairs to open up for them. They showed their warrant cards, introduced themselves and followed Laura into the lounge.

"Have you found Gayle?"

"Mrs Prendergast, may I call you Laura? The visit is a sad one for us and brings you no comfort, I'm afraid. Prepare yourself for bad news."

"Has she had an accident?"

"Gayle, your sister, has been found dead."

"Where? How? Was it near the airport?"

"She was found in the attic at your brother-in-law's property."

Laura visibly blanched. Her shoulders sank as she seemed to speak to herself.

"Oh. That was the smell then."

"The smell?"

"I visited Philip just last weekend. We were going to rack our brains to come up with other people we could contact to find out where Gayle might be. He was showing me where I would be sleeping."

"I see."

"Has he killed her? I can't believe it. I won't believe it. They're… they were such a loving couple, good friends, as well."

"Your brother-in-law is currently helping us with our enquiries. We wanted to ask you to accompany us to Stenport to identify the body."

"I'll need to let my husband know so he can pick up our daughter from school."

She leaned forward to get up from the chair and fell back again, bursting into tears. Raby found his way to the kitchen to make her a hot drink while Beryl comforted the woman.

"I'm sorry, Laura. There's no easy way of doing this. It's a dreadful shock. We are doing everything we can to find out what has happened and who has murdered her."

"I'm sorry, too. She was so clever and kind. Why would anyone want to do this?"

"Did she ever mention to you any problems she was having with Philip or anybody else?"

"No. When he first rang me with all the weird goings on about her flights and her mobile being left behind, I asked him if everything had been ok between them. His words to me were that she had been a bit standoffish before she left for Switzerland."

"And what did he say to explain that? Had they had a row?"

"He said not. He put it down to her time of the month, PMT and all that."

"Had she ever complained that he had other women?"

"No. You're joking, surely not."

Raby came in with a hot drink for Laura. She sipped and sobbed intermittently, telling the two officers about Gayle and their lives together.

"Do you feel well enough now to ring your husband? I want to take you up to Stenport while the pathologist's offices are still open. I'll come with you, and we'll follow DS Raby in his car."

Chapter 23

Beryl and Andy joined the rest of the team reviewing their progress with current cases. Laura had positively identified her sister's body. She had asked to speak to Philip, but he hadn't yet been released.

Morrison welcomed them back and invited their input to the rest. Beryl mentioned Laura's point about Gayle being standoffish from Philip before she set out for Switzerland, which he had played down as 'women's things'. Laura had thought they were happy with each other and couldn't imagine he would have killed Gayle.

Morrison mentioned Muriel Turnbill's visit to the station to make a statement following Beryl's initial visit to Stenport offices of DEFRA. He'd dealt with her while Geoff had been dispatched to collect samples of cushioning from Philip's property. Dr Dayton had reported finding the same fibres inhaled by Gayle as he had found in Margaret's body. Muriel Turnbill had been away on holiday and had just got the notification to come in and make her statement. She had given the names of two women, now moved on from Stenport, whom she knew had had flings with Philip at conferences or visits around the region. That is why she had asked Margaret whether he'd tried anything on with her when she became one of the team doing the rounds of groups affected by the foot-and-mouth outbreak. Margaret was asked to go more frequently than some of the other civil servants because she had this amazing memory for detail, which was useful to Philip Innocent who headed up that particular team.

"What did Margaret say to Muriel? Had he, or hadn't he?"

"Not then, no, but she volunteered to Muriel after Philip moved on to another job in Reychol that she had slept with him on a couple of their stayovers. Margaret said she had been at a low point with her husband Edward. She said it hadn't meant anything to Philip and he'd dropped her as soon as he left to go to EnviroOptions. So, Beryl, tomorrow I want you to get back over to Stenport and get any forward addresses for these two women."

"Right, Sir. Have you put these points to Philip Innocent yet?"

"No but we will be doing. Adam Wilson is watching the time we've had him with us in custody and is pressing us to charge him or release him. He'll be here in half an hour. He's with a client until then."

Philip was looking washed out as he took his place alongside Adam Wilson in the interview room for the third time. Morrison began with his invitation to Philip to change or add to anything he had previously said. Once again Philip denied that the evidence produced showed any involvement on his part in the murder of either woman. Morrison pressed him again.

"Can you give me the names of any other women that accompanied you or your team on regional conferences or visits over the last three years say, other than Margaret?"

"Why are you flogging this particular horse when two women have been murdered?"

"The sooner you cooperate with us, Mr Innocent, the sooner we can release you, if indeed we are going to."

"I'd need to think back. Three years with a lot happening is a long time to remember."

"Let me help you then: Felicity Graham? Kerry Gardener? Joanne Parry? Muriel Turnbill? Jean Slipman?"

"The only names I recognise from that list are Turnbill, Slipman and Gardener."

"And did all of them accompany you, singly or as a group, to a hotel for an overnight stay?"

"I recognise the Muriel Turnbill name but only as an office-based staff member. She never came away with me, as I recall."

"She may think herself fortunate in that respect. And the other two?"

"Yes. Both of them."

"Singly or together?"

"Singly, I think. What on earth has any of this got to do with Gayle or Margaret Culpebble?"

"I'm getting to that, sir. We have a statement from Muriel Turnbill that it was common knowledge around the office that both of the two women had a fling with you. What comment do you wish to make?"

"No comment, Inspector Morrison, since none of it answers who killed my wife or Margaret."

"Well then, let's get back to Margaret. Muriel Turnbill's statement says that Margaret volunteered to her that she'd slept with you at least twice before you dumped her and went off to work with your current employer. I'll ask for your comment but I think I know what your answer will be."

"It doesn't matter if she said I slept with her a hundred

times, I didn't kill her."

"Are you saying you did sleep with her?"

"I've no comment to make on that. It won't help you. You've nothing to link me to her killing, just these stories around the office which add up to nothing."

"They question your veracity as a witness, sir. We have heard from the pathologist that your wife's lungs had inhaled fibres from whatever pad or material was used to asphyxiate her. The fibres are of the same type as those found in Margaret's lungs. Have you any clever comments to make about that, sir?"

"There's nothing I would wish more than to have Gayle safe and sound. That will never happen now. I've no clever comments, as you call them, to offer you, Inspector, just my regret that this has happened to her. I want to go home. Can I see her?"

"I'm afraid not. The post-mortem is still incomplete. Your sister-in-law has been to the mortuary to identify your wife's body."

Philip's head sank into his hands.

"She told DC Gillibrand that, when you first phoned to tell her that Gayle hadn't travelled to Switzerland, she'd asked you whether your wife had been ok when you last saw her. She said you had replied that she had been a bit standoffish. Can you explain that?"

"I can't really say. I just thought she was a bit withdrawn, and she rebuffed any of my concerns, so I put it down to her monthlies. As I told you, I was due to go out to Basle for a long weekend and I hoped to find her back to her normal self again."

"Even while she was lying dead in your attic?"

"I had no knowledge of that until you came to search my home and found her. You can imagine how much of a fool I felt. I'd been chasing across Basle to look for her and she was up above me all the time. I swear to you I didn't know."

Adam Wilson signalled a request for a conference outside the interview room. He asked Morrison whether he had anything other than circumstantial conjecture to hold his client further. Morrison argued that the link between the deaths of the two women was Philip Innocent. He had demonstrably lied about his association with Margaret Culpebble which put a question mark about his other stories. Forensic tests had still to be reported which he hoped would prove his suspicions. Wilson pressed again for his client to be released, since Morrison didn't have anything other than hearsay against Mr Innocent. Morrison asked for Philip's passport to be retained and for his weekly attendance at the station until he could be eliminated as a suspect. Wilson felt that Innocent would volunteer his passport to himself for a set limited period to show willing, but it was up to the investigation team to come up with more substantial evidence than had been presented so far.

Chapter 24

Philip rang the same doorbell DC Gillibrand and DS Raby had rung twenty-four hours previously. He felt uncertain, to say the least, about how his unannounced visit would be received. Laura answered the door and looked at him long and hard before acknowledging his presence.

"Why are you here, Philip?"

"I needed to see you. You had to identify Gayle's body. That should have been down to me. Can I come in? I need to talk to you."

"Have you been cleared by the police?"

"They've released me on bail with restrictions on leaving the area until all the forensic reports are in and I have been eliminated."

"So still not in the clear?"

"Please let me talk to you."

"Only if you're going to talk to me truthfully."

"I promise."

Laura led him through to the lounge. She made him some tea, and they sat facing each other across the table.

"How are you?"

"I feel very strange. They told me in the last interview that you'd been to identify Gayle's body. They won't let me see her. How was she?"

"There's no easy way to dress this up, Philip. She looked a long time dead. She had discoloured badly and there were bruise marks around her nose and mouth where the killer had held something over her face and pressed hard. And her head had been shaved."

Philip's eyes watered.

"When the two officers came to take me up to the mortuary in Stenport, they asked me questions about you and Gayle and whether she'd mentioned to me about other women in your life. Why would they put such a question to me, Philip?"

"Because they want me to be the murderer of Margaret, the woman I found dead in the woods, and Gayle. They kept saying I was the link."

"But how?"

"Because I worked with Margaret among others in the team when we were cleaning up administratively after the foot-and-mouth outbreak."

"I don't understand. Why did they focus on you? How about the other people on that job?"

"Because Margaret and I worked together on our own towards the end of the incident. Her husband, Edward, rang her in the morning of one of our overnight stays in the Lakes and said there was a man in the room with her."

"And was there, Philip? Was it you?"

"Yes."

Laura sprang from her seat and walked up and down, pushing her fists into her cheeks and chunnering expletives.

"How could you? You bastard! Why? Tell me why!"

"I wish I could give you an answer that would mean anything. I loved Gayle. I love her still. None of the women meant anything to me in any way other than a break in the boredom of my own company while Gayle was working away from home."

"You make it sound like an excuse. What about loyalty and faithfulness?"

"They were never in question. I never pestered any of them for sex. They approached me."

"Did Gayle know? Was there some arrangement between you?"

"Gayle didn't know. There was no need for her to know. It didn't occur often enough for it to become an issue."

"You think? What if she met one of them and it came out?"

"That was never going to happen."

"You're so sure of yourself, Philip. Maybe it already has. If you didn't kill Gayle, maybe some boyfriend or partner did find out and attacked Gayle to get back at you."

"It seems to me that he's more likely to come from among Gayle's clients than anyone I've worked with."

"I just don't know what to say to you. I despise what you've done."

"I understand that. I would never hurt Gayle."

"You already have, whether she knew about your other life or not. Supposing she did know and had to deal with it. That would make someone question everything about one's life with another person. You said she was – what was the word you used? – standoffish, before she left last time. Supposing someone had told her?

"I can't think who. Margaret, it seems, was already long dead when I found her in Birkacre Woods, and the other two women had left DEFRA. I still think it was one of her clients. Margaret being dead, as well, is just a random coincidence. I had nothing to do with either death."

"Have the police checked her client list?"

"Yes. Morrison told me some time ago that they were working through her files."

"Do we just sit and wait until they come up with somebody?"

"I would think that something like this takes a lot of time and manpower."

"So what about you now?"

"I spoke with my boss early this morning and he's told me to take the rest of the week off to get my head straight. He doesn't want me mucking up the stage we're at with the incinerator project. He's worried about any adverse press coverage. My job might be on the line. When I got back late last night, my answer machine was already full of requests for interviews. The police had also taken all our cushions. Morrison was telling me that both women's lungs had inhaled the same type of fibres. I'm shit-scared, after everything else that has appeared out of nowhere, that someone has planted the cushion at my house."

"How's that possible?"

"Whoever it is must have Gayle's keys. That's, in part, why I wanted to see you. If it happens that the police pick me up again, I promise you that, whatever story is fabricated against me, I did not kill Gayle."

"I have to take that on trust. Have you done anything about changing your locks?"

"I was ringing firms this morning before I drove down here."

"How about a camera or an alarm? Do you have one?"

"No, but I'm going to discuss some set-up with the chap coming tomorrow afternoon. Getting the locks changed will be the security measure I can get done soonest. Anything else might be closing the stable door after the horse has bolted."

"What about your neighbours? Have you had a chance to talk to them?"

"I was taken into the station immediately they found Gayle's body. The police will have been round the estate. I'll have to do the same; find out if anybody has been seen, hanging around."

" You said a cushion might have been planted, among other things. What kind of things?"

"Apart from the spends on her card, which anybody who had stolen it might have made, it struck me that they were aimed at Gayle or me: flight in my name, hotel stay in my name. The expenditure wasn't for clothing or household items or music. The spender didn't obviously benefit himself, well, up to the point that the card was stopped. And then there were the letters – one sent from me to Margaret I never wrote and one from Margaret to me I never received."

"Where were they found?"

"The one I was supposed to have sent was among Margaret's books, and the DS searching my home, when I was taken away to the police station, found her letter to me in a file I had on the Birkacre Woods project. That had to have been planted. Why not any of the other projects I have been involved with? It feels like an after-the-event act."

"What do you mean?"

"Well, Margaret's body had been found. Maybe it wasn't meant to be found when it was, so the killer had to build up evidence away from him and on to me."

"But why, if the deaths are coincidental, like you said?"

"I think I've just worked out what the police have been saying all along. Except they are missing the point. I wouldn't be the first to be charged on trumped-up evidence. Getting a case solved quickly is beneficial for the police. I look very suspicious to them at the moment. They only need some forensic result to point the finger at me, and I'm sunk."

"Is that likely?"

"Not directly."

"What do you mean?"

"Well, since I didn't murder either Gayle or Margaret, there wouldn't be anything to link with me. The poster I saw of Margaret showed her with her head shaved. When I was at the scene with the police, what was revealed, apart from a corset of some kind, was bare. I wonder if Gayle's body was, too. You said her head had been shaved."

"Yes, but I don't know if she was found without clothing. I wasn't told and I didn't think to ask. It was all such a shock."

"She wouldn't have had any jewellery on her. I found that around the house. I didn't think she was in the habit of leaving it behind when she was away working, but I honestly can't be sure. The same with her phone. So anything that leads the police to me has to follow a trail to me, like the letters. That's why I have this awful feeling that one of the cushions they've lifted from our house will turn out to be the one used to asphyxiate both Gayle and Margaret. It will lead straight to me, don't you see?"

"And you think that's going to happen?"

"Why wouldn't it? The killer wants me to be charged and sent to court."

"Do you now mean that the two murders are linked?"

"The more I think about it, yes."

"If somebody knew you were involved with Margaret, that would account for her death as an act of revenge. But what about Gayle's murder? How do you link that with Margaret's? Who knew Margaret and Gayle?"

"Edward, Margaret's husband, would be a likely suspect for her murder. The only thing that could obviously connect him with Gayle is that he must have been a client at her clinic."

"Do you know if the police have interviewed him like they have you?"

"When I was being interviewed, I asked Morrison that. I asked him whether Edward was one of Gayle's clients, but he said not. What I want to do is get a photo of Edward Culpebble and show it to staff at the clinic and around my neighbours to see if he is the link and not me."

"Ok. How can I help?"

"I don't know how long forensic tests will take. Since it's key to both cases, the police will probably want them to go to the top of the list. If I use the time this week to watch his house and grab a shot, can I ask you to show it around the clinic and neighbours, if I get re-arrested?"

"I'll need to talk it over with David but I think that should be ok. He's no feelings either way about your involvement. He was waiting to see if the police would release you… Look at the time! Listen! I have to go and collect Lily from school. She'll be wondering whether I've forgotten her. Are you coming with me or staying here, or what?"

"Thanks all the same, but I think my freedom to act is on borrowed time, so I'll drive back and get over to Culpebble's place. Thanks for listening to me, Laura. I didn't think you'd even let me through the door."

"I nearly didn't. But, Philip, I remind you, your claim

that you didn't kill Gayle is on trust."

"And I will honour that trust, I promise you."

Chapter 25

From his position parked up in a short cul-de-sac at the end of Culpebble's estate, Philip faced his third day of enforced boredom waiting to get any appearance of Edward Culpebble recorded by his camera.

He'd missed an opportunity the previous afternoon, only catching, at the last minute, the back view of Edward's car disappearing into his garage. After hours of waiting, Philip had got engrossed in the newspaper's crossword and only realised, too late, that Edward's car had arrived in his drive. He had thrown the paper aside but fumbled picking up his camera. His resulting image was nothing that could be shown to anybody to identify Edward Culpebble. He had fumed at his lack of focus, both personal and technical, and he began to question whether there was any point in his present purpose. After sitting through further hours of decreasing light and increasing numbness in his buttocks, he had decided to call it a day. In passing Edward's house he noted, with Edward's car sitting this time on his drive, that they both drove BMW cars of a similar make and colour. He slowed down and took a picture of the car with its number plate.

Today he felt hopeful of some success when he had

seen Edward's car still parked up on the drive, having arrived early to catch the man leaving for work. He had begun to wonder whether the man worked from home or didn't go out to work at all for some reason when the car was still sitting at gone eleven am. He'd seen the postman's van come and leave, to his regret, without any visit to Edward's address.

A half an hour later he sat up with renewed expectation when he saw a delivery van draw up at the end of Edward's drive. He raised his camera, adjusted the zoom function and tried to slow down his breathing as the delivery man approached Edward's door. There was a delay while this was opened, but his luck kicked in when Edward stepped out to sign for his parcel, chat briefly with the man and then wait glorious seconds while the delivery man bent to pick up the parcel and hand it over safely to Edward. Philip clicked furiously, as if his life depended on it.

He watched the van leave then assessed his images. He nearly wept with joy when he saw two or three that would stand scrutiny. He phoned Laura and shared his excitement with her. He discussed his plan to print the best of his shots, email copies to her as a failsafe and pay a visit to Mrs Cavendish's clinic. So far so good.

Chapter 26

"It's very kind of you, Mrs Cavendish, to spare me your time. I know you must be busy."

"Please, Mr Innocent – may I call you Philip? – don't mention it. I'm pleased to have an opportunity to say to you personally how sorry we all are to read about Gayle's awful death. She will be badly and sadly missed by us, her colleagues, and I anticipate we will be receiving condolences from many people associated with the clinic, some clients included, I have no doubt. How can I be of help?"

"The press, thankfully, don't have all the details yet, but I need to be honest with you, Mrs Cavendish, and say that I have been questioned by the police and released."

"I see."

"Gayle's body was found in our attic. I would like you to keep that to yourself. The press will be getting on to you when they find out that she worked here."

"I imagine it won't take long, particularly in view of the work we do here."

"Quite! I need your help with one of Gayle's clients."

"Why is that, Philip?"

"You've very kindly not asked me whether I killed Gayle. Someone is trying to make out that I killed her and the other woman found dead in Birkacre Woods."

"Go on."

"I worked with that lady when I was at DEFRA and I was the one who found her body –not knowing it was her at the time-when I was doing a check for the trustees."

"What an awful coincidence!"

"While I was out and about trying to find Gayle after she'd gone missing, someone gained access to our house. I think someone killed Gayle and used her keys to get her body into the attic and leave things around that would incriminate me and lead the police to me as the killer. I told you I'd been held by the police. I have a great fear they will come back for me. That's why I need your help urgently."

"This all sounds very strange. What do you want me to do?"

Philip reached into his case and drew out some of the photos he'd taken of Edward Culpebble. He fanned them out on the desk in front of Mrs Cavendish.

"Do you recognise this man?"

Mrs Cavendish studied the pictures carefully, shaking her head slowly.

"I'm sorry, Philip. I can't say I've ever seen him before. Do you think he was one of Gayle's clients?"

"I'm counting on it. It's the only thing that makes sense about this hell I've found myself in."

"The police have been and checked through her files."

"DI Morrison told me that already, but I think this man may have used a different name to the one he is normally known by."

"He's not someone I've seen here."

171

"Is it in order for me to ask your receptionist?"

"I'll call her in."

Mrs Cavendish dialled through to Mrs Jepson and asked her to join them.

Philip visibly deflated when Mrs Jepson's response to the photos was the same as that of Mrs Cavendish.

"Is there anyone else who would deal with clients?"

Mrs Jepson volunteered that their other receptionist, Miss Lester, would be the only other person to approach.

"Can we call her in?"

"I'm sorry, Philip. Miss Lester is taking some leave this week."

"Can I call her or email her? It's so important. I'm sure you'll agree, Mrs Cavendish."

"It's our policy not to release contact details of our staff, Philip. Don't look so crestfallen. I was going to say that we'll contact her and get her to make some arrangement to check the photos for you. Do you want to leave me one?"

"You promise you'll ring her? My life depends on it."

"That's a bit dramatic, Philip."

"I mean it. I think I'm going to be stitched up for two murders that I swear to you I didn't commit."

"What are you going to do if Miss Lester does come in but doesn't recognise this man either?"

"Then I think I will be well and truly sunk."

"Let's hope it doesn't come to that. Mrs Jepson, will you give Miss Lester a call? Tell her to contact the clinic urgently, if you have to leave a message."

While Mrs Jepson was out of the room, Philip gave Mrs Cavendish his contact details and those for Gayle's sister, as well, in the event he was re-arrested by the police. He advised that Laura had copies of the photos should Miss Lester be unable to get into the clinic. Mrs Jepson returned after five minutes and said the number she'd rung had gone straight to voicemail. The message had been left as per instruction.

Philip hung on at the clinic until it closed at six, in the hope that Miss Lester would make contact. He waited in vain.

Chapter 27

On her way home, Mrs Cavendish took a longer route along the M66 to call at Barbara's address. The family were just finishing their evening meal. They invited her in and offered her some tea. She declined the hospitality and asked instead if she might speak to Barbara. Mrs Lester apologised that Bowie wasn't in the house. She was supposed to be staying for her week's break at her friend's flat in Elston near Stenport. They'd had a call from her to say the friend had been taken ill and was being kept in hospital for observation. Bowie was staying on to visit her friend and be around to help when she was discharged from hospital.

Mrs Cavendish explained that she was trying to contact Barbara about an important administrative issue but that her phone had been switched off. She asked if she might have the number for the friend's flat. Mrs Lester went to check their address book and returned with the details. Having said her goodbyes to Barbara's mother, Mrs Cavendish got back into her car and tried the number for the flat in Elston. It answered on the sixth ring.

"Hello."

"Hello, Barbara, is that you? It's Jean Cavendish."

"Oh hello, Mrs Cavendish. Is there a problem?"

"I've just been talking with your mother. We've been trying to ring you from the clinic this afternoon but your phone was switched off."

"Oops! Let me just check… I had it switched off while I was visiting my friend. She's had to go into hospital and I was with her this afternoon."

"Yes. Your mother explained all that. I hope your friend is on the mend."

"They kept her in for observation at Stenport Infirmary and I'm going to stay here to help her get back on her feet after they discharge her over the next day or so. What's the matter at the clinic?"

"Well, you know I wouldn't normally be ringing you at home, but Dr Innocent's husband came in to see me this afternoon. He was most anxious to identify a man he thought might have been a client of Gayle's. Both Mrs Jepson and I couldn't recognise the man in Philip's photos, and he asked if he could show the photos to you. I explained you were on leave, but he's in a bit of a state, understandably with the death of his wife."

"I know. It's awful. I couldn't believe it when I saw the paper."

"Awful, as you say. He told me this strange story of being taken in by the police for questioning, being interviewed and then released but feeling they'll be back for him. He says someone has been getting into their house and leaving items to incriminate him. He says he's at his wits' end."

"That must be a nightmare. I could meet him somewhere in Stenport after visiting hours tomorrow afternoon. Would that help?"

"I won't be able to be with you, Barbara. I'm in conference over in Sheffield tomorrow."

175

"I'll be alright. If I meet him somewhere public?"

"Have you your computer with you? We could check the photo that way. I can email you my copy tonight."

"That wouldn't be any good. I didn't bring it with me. We planned to have a cyber-free week."

"Let me think. I'd feel happier if you had somebody with you. Mr Innocent said his sister-in-law, Gayle's older sister had copies of the photos, too, just in case he was re-arrested. If I give you Mr Innocent's phone number, you could arrange something with him and insist Gayle's sister comes along, as well."

"It's alright, really."

"No, Barbara. Be advised on this. I don't want to get back from Sheffield and find out an important member of my staff has gone missing in Stenport."

"Are you saying he's dangerous?"

"In all honesty, no, but better to be ultra careful than sorry."

"Ok. Give me the number then. I'll try and get in touch."

Mrs Cavendish spelt out the contact details to Barbara that Philip Innocent had given her, both for himself and Laura Prendergast.

Chapter 28

Philip waited impatiently for Laura to pick up.

"Hi. It's me, Philip. Mrs Cavendish, Gayle's boss, has helped me to find the woman who could, maybe, identify the man in my photos… Yes. I was in with her today. Miss Lester, that's the name of the receptionist, is on leave this week but Mrs C got her to contact me. I'm just finished speaking with her."

"Is she going to meet you at the clinic?"

"No. That's the problem. She's flatsitting for a friend who's gone into hospital in Stenport. We've arranged to meet up in the café of a department store near the Infirmary. Miss Lester, I think Mrs C said she was called Barbara, will nip across from visiting her friend."

"When will you be meeting?"

"She's suggested 2 p.m. after early visiting hours, but, another thing, Laura, she won't meet me unless you're there, as well. Mrs C has advised her to ask you to come along, too, or there'll be no show."

"I see."

"Mrs C would do it but she's in Sheffield at a

conference tomorrow. Will you be able to come?"

"It sounds like I'll have to. Let me get something to write on… Fire away. What's the name of the store and where is it in Stenport?"

"It's the café on the first floor of Unsworth's Department store on Lancaster Road. There's a car park over the top two floors of the building."

"So, 2 p.m., you say? How will we know who this Barbara Lester is among any of the other customers?"

"She says she'll be wearing one of those quilted jackets. It's a mink colour. What's that? Light brown? Yeah, and she's fair-haired."

"Will she be wearing a white carnation?"

"I don't care what she's wearing, as long as she can identify our Mr Culpebble as one of Gayle's clients."

The doorbell rang. There was shouting.

"Open up! Police!"

Philip looked through the window and saw the police car on his drive.

"Laura. They're back. Do this for me, will you, if I'm going to be held overnight? Wish me luck. I'm frightened."

The knocking became loud and insistent.

"Open up, Mr Innocent!"

"I'll have to go, Laura. I don't want them breaking the door down."

Philip went to open the door. Morrison stood waiting, his warrant card on display. He had DS Raby and Constable Winch in support.

"Philip Innocent. I'm arresting you for the murders of Margaret Culpebble and your wife, Gayle Innocent. You may not wish to…"

Philip let him finish his script.

"You're making a huge mistake. I'll come with you, if you'll promise to listen to me."

"Oh we're going to be listening to you, Mr Innocent! Cuff him, Andy!"

Having been booked in again, Philip was led to the interview room. The routine had become less daunting after his three previous visits but he was no less uneasy about the purpose behind it.

The two detectives, Morrison and Raby, waited while Adam Wilson, the solicitor, arrived and conferred with his client. They then entered the room themselves, seeming confident and assured that they now had their man.

"Mr Innocent. You have been arrested following the results of forensic tests on fibres taken from cushion material found in our search of your property. Those tests confirm that this cushion was used to asphyxiate Margaret Culpebble and your wife, Gayle. What have you to say?"

DS Raby showed the cushion to Philip and his solicitor.

"I knew this was going to happen. I have been waiting for you to come back for me. It was just a matter of the time taken to complete the tests. I wish to say in the strongest possible terms that this cushion does not belong either to myself or Gayle. Where was it found?"

"It was collected from the upstairs rear bedroom next to the bathroom."

"There weren't any cushions upstairs. We only had cushions downstairs. This is something else that has been secreted in my house to incriminate me. Gayle's phone, her jewellery, letters, even, heaven help me, her body… they've all been placed about the house by someone who killed my wife and gained access with her keys."

"As you say, Mr Innocent. Once again, I have to ask

you how that person had links with your wife? All along you have lied to us. Why should we believe you now?"

"In the face of the evidence against me, I can understand why you think I'm guilty but I swear to you on my life that I did not kill Gayle, nor Margaret Culpebble. I've spent this week since I was released, trying to put together the evidence to convince you that I've been put in the spotlight unjustifiably, to cover up the fact that another man is guilty of these awful murders. When you called, I was arranging with Gayle's sister, Laura Prendergast, to meet one of the Cavendish clinic staff who's up in Stenport. I was going to show her photographs I'd taken and ask her if the man in them had been one of Gayle's clients."

"Who is this man, Mr Innocent?"

"Margaret Culpebble's husband, Inspector Morrison. I think Edward Culpebble was one of Gayle's clients."

"Have you shown these photographs to any of the other staff at the clinic?"

"Yes."

"And did they give you the answer you were hoping for?"

"No. Neither Mrs Cavendish, nor a part-time receptionist, a Mrs Jepson, could recognise him as ever being at the clinic."

"So your theory isn't going to save you, sir."

"Not here, no, but, if you'll give me the last chance to prove it to you, I'll take you to meet Miss Barbara Lester. She's the full-time receptionist at the Cavendish clinic and she's up in Stenport, staying with a friend who's gone into the infirmary there. She's offered to meet me tomorrow along with my sister-in-law."

"And if Miss Lester, too, is unable to confirm you in your theorising?"

"Then what hope have I got left?"

"For me to consider your proposition, Mr Innocent, is asking me to invest an inordinate amount of trust, where there's been little evidence that you are trustworthy. For what reason would Edward Culpebble murder your wife? You have repeatedly denied that there was ever any sexual relationship between you and Margaret Culpebble which might have led to a vengeful, malicious act against your wife. So I ask you again. Why would Edward Culpebble murder your wife? What would be his motive?"

Philip looked at Morrison and then at his solicitor, Adam Wilson. He nodded at Philip to go ahead. Philip weighed his answer carefully. There was a tension in the moment, as everyone waited for his reply. The faint buzz from the machine recording the interview seemed amplified in the expectant silence among the four people sitting facing each other across the table.

"I haven't been truthful in my replies about Margaret Culpebble and how we spent time together while working on the foot-and-mouth follow-up. I didn't pester her for sex. She propositioned me. I didn't write the letter to her saying 'the fun' that was mentioned in the letter was over, though I did let her know that I was moving on, both literally to a new job and metaphorically in that I wouldn't be seeing her again. While I was coming to you for help finding my wife, I became aware that you were treating me as a suspect for both killings. You will say that I have been very naïve and stupid in denying that Margaret and I had slept together on and off, but I was trying to protect myself. If I'd admitted it, I would have become the link you were looking for and I am not that person who's murdered two women."

"You're wrong in that thinking, Mr Innocent. Neither myself nor DC Gillibrand were confirmed in our belief that you were the killer. We only became so when you continued to lie. You have wasted police time and put yourself in the frame for two murders. There is nothing in what you have said that changes our position on that. Forensic evidence gained from material taken from your property adds weight to our suspicions. It's easy to say, after it's been found, that the cushion didn't belong at your address. We have hundreds of people we interview who try the same ploy of denying that evidence gained against them has anything to do with them."

"Is one day going to make such a difference?"

"Police time is very costly, Mr Innocent."

"But to make the difference between sending somebody to prison who didn't kill and letting off the hook someone who, I'm certain, did kill?"

"We have no name from among your wife's clients that matches Edward Culpebble."

"But I think he has used another name in gaining access time with my wife, Inspector, and Barbara Lester is the one person left who could tell you that. Mrs Cavendish said you'd been through Gayle's files. Are you satisfied that all the people she saw have been accounted for?"

"Mr Innocent, this is an ongoing investigation."

"Well then! Just let me meet Miss Lester this one time to resolve it forever."

"You're not going anywhere, sir. You have been taken into custody and will remain with us while we build our case against you for the Prosecution Service."

Chapter 29

Steph perked up considerably when Bowie told her that her parents had been in touch to say they were coming back from their holiday in Spain. They would be able to meet up with her after her release from hospital the following morning. Bowie checked that Steph had all the clothes she would need to go home in, before saying goodbye to her friend and making her way across town to Lancaster Road.

Morrison called Geoff Waller into his office. Having briefed the team on the previous evening's developments, he decided to send DC Waller across to Stenport to meet the two women. If Miss Lester failed to recognise Philip Innocent's photo of Edward Culpebble, that would put the case to bed. If she did, well, that would open up the case in an entirely new direction.

Morrison had sent Beryl Gillibrand off to organise a fresh warrant to search Culpebble's place in the event of a positive ID. He didn't expect it but thought it wise to be prepared.

Laura had left Hadfield in good time to make Stenport by half one. The drive along the A540 was reasonably straightforward at this time of day and the switch to the M60 Manchester Ringroad equally problem-free. She signalled her access to the M61, in order to head north to Stenport. Coming up to Junction 5, she saw a caution alert for a build-up of traffic at Junction 8. She hoped this was a message that hadn't yet cleared though the reason for it would have. As she approached Junction 8 that hope proved false, as she reacted on her brake pedal to the intensification of red lights ahead of her across the three lanes of the motorway. She looked at the time and groaned. It was twelve thirty. If the build-up didn't clear quickly, she was going to be late.

Bowie climbed up to the café on the first floor at Unsworth's. It was busy. She hummed to herself as she looked at the menu. She decided on something light – a bacon, brie and cranberry toastie with salad and some tea while she waited for Laura Prendergast and Gayle Innocent's husband to arrive. The lady at the till took her order and payment and gave her an order pennant to stand on her table. Bowie chose a vacant spot facing the door to the café. It was a quarter past one. She checked her phone for messages and then watched the traffic and bustle of Stenport going on below her. The fine, warm weather had given way to something more showery and cool. The waitress brought her order, and Bowie tucked into her toastie, relishing the sharpness of the cranberry that had softened the crispness of the heated bread. She looked across to the queue which was easing off as the lunch hour rush came to its conclusion. She checked her watch. It was coming up to two. She looked again expectantly at the door for any man and woman arriving together. She finished her toastie and poured the last of the tea from the pot. She looked up again and saw a man by himself join the short queue. She had a déjà vu suggestion of familiarity about him. She looked once again at the door for any new arrivals.

Laura began to feel a tension develop in her body as she tried to resist the instinct to build up speed to shorten the last part of her journey to Stenport. Filtering three lanes of motorway traffic into one, to negotiate round an accident just before Junction 8 exit, had taken an hour. People with important business were reluctant to give way, and the traffic police had had to instil some organisation into the process. She finally parked up in Unsworth's car park at twenty past two.

She oriented herself towards the stairs to the lower floors and got down them as fast as she could, hoping Miss Lester would still be there. She barged through the entrance to the café and cast around for a young, fair-haired woman wearing a light brown quilted jacket. Nobody she could see bore any resemblance. A tall, slim man was standing in front of a table. She wondered if he were talking to someone sitting there. She edged to one side to get an unobscured view and saw the young, fair-haired woman in the expected jacket with her head tilted at an uncomfortable angle, looking up at the tall man talking to her. She approached the table and her introduction came out in a breathless, garbled rush.

"Hello. Miss Lester? I'm late. I'm sorry. I'm Laura. I've come on my own."

She stopped and took in the features of the man who turned towards her, curious to know who had interrupted. A strange apprehension took hold of her body and she felt the hairs stand up on the back of her neck. She felt the primeval urge for flight but dared an approach to the man whose face she recognised from the photos she was carrying.

"Is this your father, Miss Lester?"

She reached out to shake his hand.

"My name is Laura Prendergast. I'm Gayle Innocent's sister."

He made no responding gesture. Laura caught the most infinitesimally small flicker of malice in his eyes.

"Excuse me, ladies. I have to go. I'll leave you to it."

The man moved quickly to the café entrance and was gone.

"Who was that?"

Barbara, Bowie Lester explained how she'd noticed him come to the counter and had vaguely remembered seeing him before. He'd stopped at her table on the way out to say hello. She'd recognised him from the clinic. He was saying how sorry he'd been to hear about Dr Innocent's death in the papers and wanted to pass on his condolences to the clinic staff.

Laura fished in her bag for the wallet of photos and asked Barbara if she recognised the man in them and knew his name.

"Yes that's the same man. He was one of Dr Innocent's clients. DC Waller asked me about him some time ago. It's a Mr McCord. He became a client in March just before Dr Innocent went to Switzerland. The police had been checking all her files and interviewing the clients. They hadn't been able to locate that man and wanted a description. Is there something wrong?"

Laura quickly explained the reason for their meeting and why she'd had to come without Philip. She told Barbara the man she'd met at the clinic as a Mr McCord was, in fact, Edward Culpebble and how they needed to inform Belton police ASAP because he could have killed Gayle and his own wife, as well.

Barbara seemed seized by a moment of shock but collected herself and searched in her bag for her mobile. She explained that she had the contact number for DC Waller and would ring him, even as she was scrolling down her screen for his number. He answered just as he'd finished paying for his parking ticket two floors up from where Barbara was calling him. Laura asked to speak to him. She confirmed that Barbara had identified Edward Culpebble as a Mr McCord, a client of Gayle's from just before she was to have left for Switzerland; how he'd just been in the café talking to Barbara when she herself had arrived and how he'd made off sharpish when she'd introduced herself as Gayle's sister. She gave him the description and registration of his car from another of the photos she'd brought with her. She urged the likelihood that he could be collecting his car from the store's upper parking.

Geoff Waller asked Laura to take Barbara Lester up to Belton Police Station to give statements while he alerted Morrison to get a team down to Culpebble's address.

Chapter 30

Geoff Waller ended his call with Laura and, as he was keying in Morrison's contact number to alert him, he realised there were two parking floors. He got out of his car and scanned the level he was at for anyone arriving to pick up their vehicle or pull away. Morrison answered as Geoff negotiated the steps down to the lower level. He briefed Morrison on developments and his current search for Culpebble's car. Morrison told Geoff to find and stick with Culpebble's vehicle. He would dispatch Andy and Beryl with the warrant to Culpebble's address. Geoff should join them there for arrest and full house search. The forensics team would be there later on. Geoff walked along the lines of parked cars on this level, hunting for Culpebble's silver BMW. He returned to the upper parking bays. He turned back on himself in response to an ear-piercing screech of tyres in the low-roofed area and saw the boot of a silver BMW negotiating the tight bend of the exit ramp. He raced to his own car and worked his way down the two ramps to the exit on to Lancaster Road. He saw Culpebble's car sitting among other cars at the traffic lights a hundred yards further on, as he fiddled with the ticket to gain his own exit.

He followed the stream of traffic heading west out of

Stenport to pick up the A59 to Botswortham. He hung back as cars dropped out of the flow of traffic. He followed the BMW as it turned right, into the estate that he remembered visiting to collect a letter. Culpebble had left his car's engine running and the driver's door open. He was in an almighty hurry. Geoff knew the small estate could only be accessed and exited from this point of entry, so he sat waiting for his two colleagues to arrive, ready to cut off Culpebble's escape. After twenty-five minutes their unmarked car arrived and blocked the exit to Culpebble's drive. Geoff walked to join his two colleagues, as they entered the property through the front door standing wide open. Geoff switched off the BMW's engine, took the keys and locked the car. He heard voices shouting at different levels within the property as Beryl and Andy searched for Edward Culpebble. Geoff closed the front door and checked that the back door was secure against escape. He heard Beryl upstairs calling Edward's name to come out of what must have been a locked bathroom. Andy ran outside through to the back of the property to check upper windows. The bathroom window was too small to get out of. He rejoined Geoff and the two made their way upstairs to corner Culpebble. Before they reached the return of the stair, a loud shriek from Beryl was followed by the sound of a scuffle as she tried to hang on to Edward vacating the bathroom in a final lunge to get clear. Edward bowled into the two men, knocking Andy off-balance but coming to an exhausted stop against Geoff who had dropped back down the stairs and squared off his body to take the force of Edward's jump down the last two stairs. Geoff rotated Edward's body and dropped it on the hall carpet, kneeling into his back.

"Edward Culpebble, I am arresting you…"

Laura and Barbara presented themselves at Belton Police Station and were led through to interview rooms for statements to be taken.

Morrison took a call from Geoff telling him the arrest had been made and, from a search of immediate personal effects, they had found a credit card with Gayle Innocent's name on it. Andy would wait to give forensic teams access, and Beryl and he would bring Culpebble up to Belton.

Morrison thanked Barbara and Laura for their significant help in moving the case on.

Laura had wanted to stay and see Philip, but Morrison said there were still things to do before Philip would be released. He would organise a lift for him. Laura offered then to see Barbara safely back to Elston before her own homeward journey.

While he was finalising the paperwork for Philip's release, Beryl Gillibrand had phoned Morrison to get Philip to check the suitcase they had in the evidence store.

Better now was her thinking than dragging him back in, once Edward Culpebble's interviews were underway.

Philip took in the starkness of the imagery as he entered the interview room, where the black suitcase, resting on the table, seemed to be the only solid object in this space. Morrison invited them both to wear gloves while the case was opened and the few contents pored over. Philip lifted a short-sleeved blouse and imagined a happier time when Gayle had been wearing it. He indicated to Morrison two such blouses and some underwear he had bought Gayle as a Valentine's gift this very year.

With forms completed and personal items restored and signed for, Philip followed Morrison to the staff car park. During the journey to Philip's address in Mellor Green, Morrison outlined Philip's likely involvement as a witness in the case that would now be built against Edward Culpebble. Much of Morrison's advice to Philip went unabsorbed. His mind skitted back and forth over the events of this last week and the unreality of it all. He felt sheer relief that Edward Culpebble had been recognised and that he himself had been released.

Epilogue

Laura arrived back in Hadfield late on Friday evening. The warmth of David's hug and his "Hi, sugar. How did you get on?" opened the sluice gates to the build-up of stress and emotion that she had been containing. They stood in the hall wrapped in each other's embrace. Lily emerged from the kitchen to greet her mum and join in.

With Lily finally in bed, Laura and David talked into the early hours about what would unfold in the coming months. Laura had phoned Philip but his phone had been switched off.

Late Saturday afternoon saw Bowie taking the bus home to Hollinbury. Steph's mum and dad had made it from Manchester airport to her flat in Elston an hour after the two young women had got back from the hospital.

On Saturday evening, after all the details of Friday's drama had been told to the members of her family, she took a call from Geoff Waller who thanked her for her help and expressed the hope that he might see more of her once the case had gone to trial.

In another place Beryl Gillibrand took the plastic wrapping from the disc which she inserted into the machine to start the recording. Morrison detailed the preliminaries and set out the charges for Edward Culpebble to address.

"Mr Culpebble. Can you explain to us how you came to be in possession of Gayle Innocent's bank card…?"

Sitting in his lounge after breakfast, Philip felt down the side of the armchair from where he had first retrieved Gayle's phone. With his eyes fixed on a photograph of her, he listened to the silence of the house. The euphoria of Friday evening's release from custody was warped by the sense of emptiness that he inhabited today, that would envelop him tomorrow and, as he saw it at that moment, would be with him for the rest of his life.

55855847R00111

Made in the USA
Charleston, SC
10 May 2016